10 INDIAN HEROES

WHO HELP PEOPLE LIVE WITH DIGNITY

SOMAK GHOSHAL

Read more in the 10s series

10 Indian Animals You May Never Again See in the Wild
by Ranjit Lal

10 Indian Monarchs Whose Amazing Stories You May Not Know
by Devika Rangachari

10 Indian Women Who Were the First to Do What They Did
by Shruthi Rao

10 Indian Champions Who Are Fighting to Save the Planet
by Bijal Vachharajani and Radha Rangarajan

10 INDIAN HEROES WHO HELP PEOPLE LIVE WITH DIGNITY

SOMAK GHOSHAL

An imprint of Penguin Random House

For Tintin, hoping he will read this book one day

PENGUIN BOOKS

USA | Canada | UK | Ireland | Australia
New Zealand | India | South Africa | China | Singapore

Duckbill Books is part of the Penguin Random House group of companies
whose addresses can be found at global.penguinrandomhouse.com

Published by Penguin Random House India Pvt. Ltd
4th Floor, Capital Tower 1, MG Road,
Gurugram 122 002, Haryana, India

Penguin
Random House
India

First published in Duckbill Books by
Penguin Random House India 2021

Text copyright © Somak Ghoshal 2021

Somak Ghoshal asserts the moral right to be
identified as the author of this work.

10 9 8 7 6 5 4 3 2

The views and opinions expressed in this book are the author's own and the
facts are as reported by him which have been verified to the extent possible, and
the publishers are not in any way liable for the same.

ISBN 9780143450979

For sale in the Indian subcontinent only

Typeset in Sitka by DiTech Publishing Services Pvt. Ltd

Printed at Manipal Technologies Limited, India

www.penguin.co.in

MIX
Paper | Supporting
responsible forestry
FSC® C043100

This is a legitimate digitally printed version of the book and therefore might not
have certain extra finishing on the cover.

10

INTRODUCTION: D IS FOR DIGNITY   1

THE LONELY FIGHTER   4

THE RIGHT TO KNOW   14

THE FIGHT TO END THE WORST 'JOB'
IN THE WORLD   23

A RIVER AND ITS PEOPLE   32

THE HEALER OF DAMAGED HEARTS   41

THE FIGHT FOR SAFE WORKPLACES   50

THE RIGHT TO LOVE   60

ABOLISHING THE DEATH PENALTY   70

THE VICTIMS OF THE BHOPAL
GAS TRAGEDY   79

BELIEF IN ABILITY   88

INTRODUCTION: D IS FOR DIGNITY

The idea of dignity is at the core of our identity as Indians. In 1949, when the Constitution was adopted under the leadership of Babasaheb Ambedkar, the word was introduced into the Preamble—in the very first sentences of this document by which the entire nation is expected to conduct itself. While promising equality, liberty and justice, 'We, the people of India' made a pledge to secure for all citizens 'fraternity assuring the dignity of the individual.' This is a powerful sentiment, and you may have heard these words being recited aloud in late 2019 and the early months of 2020, when people came out on the streets of Indian cities in big numbers to protest against a law that would grant Indian citizenship selectively to people of all religions except Islam.

But what does dignity really mean? How do you experience it in your daily life? And, more importantly, what does it look like in practice, as opposed to simply being an idea in our minds?

The aim of this book is to try answering these questions through the stories of ten individuals, who put themselves out in the world to fight for dignity for everyone—no matter how rich or poor, old or young, familiar or different, they may be. The English word 'dignity' comes from the Latin *dignitas*, which refers to a state of being worthy. The ten crusaders of dignity in this book argue, following the principles laid out in the Constitution, that every human being is worthy of being treated with respect, honour, compassion and courtesy—all the codes of conduct we associate with 'dignity'.

I picked these ten heroes because their work speaks to me urgently—but there are hundreds of others like them, dead or living, who have made it their mission to fight for human rights. If you read the chapters carefully, you will also see that although each one is tied to the life and work of one person, in reality, they could not have done what they do without the support of a host of other people around them. In a sense, therefore, their stories are also celebrations of the power of the collective and the beauty of unified action. It is also important to remember that a short book like this cannot do justice to a vast and complex topic like dignity. But if, after reading it, you are inspired to seek out more information about human rights, and about many others who fight for it every day of their lives, I would consider my job done.

What these stories, I hope, will show you is that there is enormous injustice around us that we fail to notice, or casually turn our eyes away from—and, equally, there are people around us who refuse to ignore such daily indignities. These fighters for human rights will do anything to go the distance—be it refusing to eat for years, leading peaceful protests, organizing the communities around them, or educating the poor and illiterate—to see that the promises made in the

Constitution by the founding fathers and mothers of independent India are fulfilled.

If you are inspired to take some steps of your own—whether by standing up against a school bully or learning to express gratitude for the people who keep our homes and cities clean—after reading about the giant strides taken by these ten heroes, the purpose of this book will have been served.

Somak Ghoshal,
Bengaluru-Mysore, March 2021

THE LONELY FIGHTER

Irom Sharmila
b. 1972

On 2 November 2000, a twenty-eight-year-old woman in the north-eastern state of Manipur was keeping a fast. She had fasted every Thursday since she was a young girl; little did she know that this habit of hers would change the course of her life before that particular day was over.

Irom Sharmila had been a gentle and quiet child. Born on 14 March 1972, in a town called Kongpal near Imphal, the capital of Manipur, she was the youngest of nine siblings. Although she grew up in a large family, Sharmila was solitary by nature. She had a few close friends, but mostly kept to herself. At school, her grades were passable, but she rarely got into trouble. From her grandmother, Sharmila heard stories of the myths and legends associated with her community. And as she learnt about the rich history of the Manipuris, a proud and brave people, Sharmila began to realize that few traces of that once-glorious past remained in the present.

The state Sharmila grew up in had been torn by violent conflicts since India became independent. The Nagas, Kukis, Meiteis and other tribes of Manipur have been fighting with one another for many years for different reasons. One group demanded freedom from India and a separate state for itself, carved out from within Manipur. Another wanted to merge a part of Manipur with the neighbouring state of Nagaland. Unrest and mayhem spread through the region like wildfire, innocent lives were lost as insurgents clashed and unleashed havoc.

Worried about these rebel factions, the Indian government sent in the army to control the situation. The army had special powers that allowed them to detain, arrest and shoot at suspects. A law called Armed Forces (Special Powers Act), 1958, known in short as AFSPA, gave the army permission to use force and other extreme measures to bring peace and order to 'disturbed areas' of the country, such as the north-eastern states and Jammu & Kashmir. But this move, ironically, had the opposite effect. It damaged the people's trust in the rule of law in those parts and led to worse anarchy. When someone is given the power to behave as they like without any fear of consequences, they can be horribly cruel towards the weak and defenceless. That's what happened with the Indian army too.

For years, the people of Manipur and other states in Northeast India lived in constant fear of being picked up by the army for offences they were not even aware of committing. Homes were raided, people disappeared after being taken away by the jawans, citizens were shot dead in broad daylight on suspicion of being enemies of the state. They were frequently abused and humiliated. If people wished to complain against the army in a court of law, they were required to seek the permission of the central government in Delhi—which was unlikely to grant it. The laws of the land that protected citizens in other parts of the country failed to safeguard the people of Manipur.

Troubled by the daily incidents of violence around her, Sharmila resolved to join the fight for human rights early on. She decided not to continue her education beyond secondary school, though she would learn shorthand later. Happy enough to be able to read and write, she felt no need for a higher degree. No amount of persuasion from her family could change her mind. Instead, she attended rallies for the right of people to live without the fear of AFSPA—it wasn't just a passing interest for Sharmila, she was passionately invested in this mission. Soon, when she was still quite young, she came up with a striking idea to strengthen her commitment to the cause.

Until the age of ten, Sharmila had been mostly vegetarian, her brother Irom Singhajit once said in an interview. But as she grew older, she began to skip meals on Thursdays as a gesture of non-violent protest against all the cruelties around her. She had in mind the example set by MK Gandhi, who was famous for staging non-violent protests by fasting during the struggle for India's independence from British rule. He held fasting to be a form of prayer that could be invoked in order to convince warring parties to set aside their differences and live in harmony. The idea appealed to Sharmila.

On that Thursday in November 2000, while Sharmila was keeping her weekly fast, a horrific tragedy shook up Manipur. In an area called Malom, not far from her home, a few people were waiting to catch a bus. It was early evening, and a convoy of three vehicles of the 8 Assam Rifles, a battalion of the Indian army, were driving by. All of a sudden, a loud explosion shook the ground, filling the air with dust. Fearing that they were under attack, the soldiers began to shoot in panic. By the time they stopped, ten people at the bus stop were dead, including Sinam Chandramani, a sixteen-year-old boy who had won an award for bravery at the age of four in 1988 from then prime minister Rajiv Gandhi. This senseless loss of lives left all of Manipur shocked and stricken with grief.

Already distraught by the news of the violence, Sharmila was jolted the morning after when she saw a photograph of the victims in a newspaper. What was the point of her protest, she wondered, of shouting slogans on the streets? Was it futile to hope for change? Questions began to swirl around her mind. It was impossible to carry on as usual—something had to give. And so, she resolved to not eat again until the government struck down AFSPA.

Having made up her mind, Sharmila got herself a couple of boxes of her favourite pastries on 4 November. Then she sat by a pond and gorged on these treats to her heart's content. After she was done eating, she went to seek her mother's blessing to begin her fast. Once her mother, Irom Sakhi Devi, had given her approval, Sharmila announced on the following day that she would not allow a morsel of food, or even a drop of water, to pass through her lips until the black law was gone.

On the first day of her fast, Sharmila staged her hunger strike at a public shelter. She sat there holding a banner asking for AFSPA to be repealed. People hovered around her, surprised and curious. Some sat with her, offered their support. But as the sun set, the crowd began to thin and, at last, everyone went home. If Sharmila had imagined that her fellow citizens would rally behind her, as they had done for Gandhi when he fasted during the freedom struggle, she was mistaken. A few did stand by her, but most treated her like an oddity.

Five days went by. Then, on 10 November, as Sharmila became visibly weaker, the government decided to intervene. In those days, the law was such that anyone seen as trying to take their own life could be sent to jail for up to a year. Sharmila, too, was arrested and taken to the Jawaharlal Nehru Institute of Medical Sciences in Imphal and held there as an undertrial. She refused to seek bail, opting to stay in custody instead. When the doctors tried to insert a tube through her mouth that would send nutrients into her body to keep her alive, Sharmila requested them to put the tube through her nose. She did not want to violate her promise of not letting any 'food' pass through her mouth until her mission was accomplished. So fiercely determined she was to follow her self-imposed rule that Sharmila sucked on cotton wool to produce saliva and keep her mouth hydrated—she did not drink one drop of water. She cleaned her teeth with cotton and applied dry spirit on her chapped lips. Anyone who has gone without food or water for even half a day would tell you how uncomfortable it can be. Imagine going on like that for days, weeks, months, years—with no end in sight.

During the year she spent in her 'hospital jail', Sharmila was allowed only a handful of visitors. She saw very little of her family and nothing of her mother, who she met again, briefly, in 2009, when Sakhi Devi was admitted to the same hospital as her. Sharmila lived in this state of confinement with her pet guinea pigs for company for years. At the end of each term of her custody, she would be released, then arrested again after a few days. The cycle would continue, year after year. Then, in 2004, another tragedy struck Manipur.

On 11 July that year, the mutilated body of a thirty-two-year-old weaver called Thangjam Manorama was discovered near her home in Imphal. Soldiers of the 17th Assam Rifles had arrested her the night before under AFSPA. Investigations revealed that she had been raped, then shot dead. There was nothing that her family could do to seek justice, as the soldiers were protected by law. But four days after this incident, twelve Manipuri women gathered in front of Kangla fort, where the army was stationed. Taking off their clothes in grief, anger and frustration, they demonstrated against the government by holding a banner that screamed: 'Indian Army Rape Us'.

These brave women were part of a grassroots group called Meira Paibi, which was formed in 1977 to fight for the right of the people of Manipur to live with dignity. The name referred to women who marched with torches—to patrol the streets and make it safe for other women as well as to rebel against injustice. The ultimate act of selfless protest of these Meira Paibi kindled the embers of resistance in the common people of Manipur.

For the first time, people began to acknowledge the tireless sacrifice of another young woman, who, by this time, had not eaten for nearly four years. As the support around her began to swell, Sharmila took an even bolder step when she was released from custody two years later.

In October 2006, loyal supporters smuggled Sharmila out of Imphal to Delhi as she came out of jail. In Delhi, she went to Rajghat to pay tribute to her idol Gandhi, then moved to Jantar Mantar, the site of public protests in the capital, to continue with her fast.

What had so far been only a fight for Manipuris became the focus of the country's attention overnight. The national media began to write about Sharmila. Her face, wracked with pain but also full of steely determination, in spite of the tube going through the nose, became a familiar sight in newspapers and on television screens.

But soon, Sharmila was arrested by the police again and sent, this time, to the All India Institute of Medical Sciences (AIIMS) in New Delhi. The familiar routine began to play out. But this time, in custody, Sharmila sent out a petition to the President to repeal AFSPA. She met the Iranian human rights activist Shirin Ebadi, who promised to highlight her fight at the United Nations. Five months later, when she was released from AIIMS, Sharmila returned to Manipur to resume her fast, and was put back in custody promptly.

Then, in 2014, Narendra Modi became prime minister after the Bharatiya Janata Party (BJP) won the elections in a landslide victory. Around this time, a law was also tabled in the Indian Parliament, called the Mental Health Care Bill, 2013, which said that anyone who attempts to kill themselves should be treated as suffering from mental health problems rather than being considered a criminal and sent to jail. Once it became a law (in 2016), it would have a big effect on Sharmila's fast.

On 27 May 2014, on the second day of Modi's prime ministership, Sharmila wrote him a letter, appealing to remove AFSPA. She clarified she was not a supporter of any rebel party. 'Please do provide us with the basic right of being a human,' she pleaded on behalf of the people whose lives were affected by AFSPA, 'so that we can live with self-respect and dignity.' But as with the earlier United Progressive Alliance government under the

Congress Party, her words fell on the deaf ears of the BJP-led National Democratic Alliance government too.

By this time, nearly fifteen years had passed since Sharmila started her fast. She was beginning to lose hope, wondering if she should try another path. Maybe getting elected as a politician would hasten the outcome of her demands?

Sharmila's personal life had also become complicated. Around 2011, a Goan-born British man called Desmond Coutinho had begun to send letters and books to Sharmila in detention. By 2016, they were in love and had decided to get married. Sharmila's family disapproved of the match, her followers were aghast and most Manipuris were critical of her choice. They had expected her to continue fasting, win the Nobel Prize for Peace, and become a global role model—not get married and settle down to a life of boring domesticity!

Sharmila, however, acted with incredible self-confidence at this difficult juncture. Just as she had vowed to fast for the sake of the people many years ago, she decided to end her fast, too, by her own free will. Her announcement was met with anger and disappointment. Sharmila's mother was especially saddened. 'I had told her that the day AFSPA is lifted from Manipur, I will feed her the first morsel of food with my own hands,' she told journalists. But Sharmila never wished to be in the limelight or be a martyr—all she wanted was to be an ambassador of peace. Yet, like many others, she also had dreams of having a family and settling down. In interviews, she repeatedly mentioned her love of life and the joy she took in the world around her. After years of frustration as an activist, she was now determined to give party politics a chance. She wanted to win elections and become the chief minister of Manipur—it would give her a better chance to end AFSPA, she felt.

In August 2016, the historic moment finally arrived. Surrounded by her supporters, well-wishers, activists and journalists from all over the world, Sharmila broke her fast after sixteen years. As she dipped a finger in honey and put it into her mouth, her face crumpled, tears streaming down her cheeks. The same year she formed the People's Resurgence and Justice Alliance (PRJA) party to fight in the assembly elections in 2017. But her political ambitions proved short-lived.

Although Sharmila took the bold step of contesting against the three-time chief minister of Manipur, Okram Ibobi Singh, from Thoubal constituency, she got only ninety votes. The message from the people was loud and clear: Sharmila was not meant to be a political leader, she was best suited to remain a civil rights activist. It was a hard blow.

Soon after this defeat, in August 2017, Sharmila got married to Coutinho in a small, private ceremony in Kodaikanal, a hill station in Tamil Nadu. It had been a year since she had ended her fast, but her family still hadn't forgiven her. Since then, Sharmila has lived a reclusive life with her husband and her twin daughters, Nix Shakhi and Autumn Tara, who were born in 2019. Occasionally, Sharmila is spotted at rallies, almost always with her children. As the people of Manipur used to call her, she remains *mengoubi*, or 'the fair one': not only fair of complexion but also fair-minded in the way she lives and conducts herself.

In spite of her long and lonely battle, Sharmila did not succeed in ending AFSPA—but her mission did not go in vain. With her unshaken spirit, she spread 'the fragrance of peace' around her, to borrow a phrase from one of her best-known poems.

The AFSPA continues to operate in different states in India—in the Northeast, Jammu & Kashmir, Punjab, and so on. Tripura was the only state to remove the law in 2015, but Nagaland remains entirely under AFSPA, while the law is relaxed in some districts of Arunachal Pradesh and Manipur. The Supreme Court in 2016 passed a ruling that the army would be subject to legal proceedings and inquiries, if they are accused of wrong doing. In 2018, some 400 soldiers submitted a plea saying that this judgement reduced the powers granted to them under AFSPA, but the Supreme Court rejected this plea. Activists across India continue to fight for the removal of AFSPA, but the road ahead of them remains long and rocky.

THE RIGHT TO KNOW

Aruna Roy and the MKSS Collective

b. 1946

Imagine you were promised a bicycle as reward for performing well in examinations. But once you passed with flying colours, you got a cricket bat—for no rhyme or reason! Wouldn't you feel upset and betrayed? Surely, you would demand to know why the deal wasn't honoured?

Poor villagers in Rajasthan—and all over India, really—have found themselves trapped in a similar, though far more serious, situation for decades. They would toil on different projects for days, building roads or digging wells, often for far longer hours than they had been employed for. But when it was time to get paid, they were given only a fraction of the agreed wages. Their employers and contractors were always ready with one excuse or the other to justify the cuts—sometimes they didn't even care to offer any reason for denying them fair pay. Most of the villagers were not literate, or were, at best, barely educated. With limited awareness of their rights, they could not persist with their demands. Worse still, they lived in mortal fear of the upper-caste village leaders, who had oppressed them for generations and threatened them with violence for the slightest move that offended them.

Into this den of corruption and cruelty a brave woman arrived in the mid-1980s, joined by a handful of dedicated associates. Aruna Roy had been a teacher at Indraprastha College in Delhi, before joining the Indian Administrative Service. Her job had taken her into the heart of the country, to areas untouched by development, where people lived in immense difficulty, neglected by the authorities and forced to accept the injustices heaped upon them without question. Later, Roy joined Social Work and Research Centre, a voluntary agency led by her husband Bunker Roy. It opened her eyes to the sorry state of public health in the villages, the general lack of education, and the severe hardship faced especially by the women. Above all, she was shocked by the daily challenges of earning a steady livelihood that millions seemed to be struggling with in these parts.

In 1987, Roy took a radical decision. She moved to Devdungri, a tiny village in Rajasthan, to live among the locals.

Nikhil Dey, son of an air marshal with the Indian Air Force who was studying in the US, decided to drop out of college and join Roy. Concerned by the disconnect he saw in his life in the West and his desire to help the neediest in his home country, Dey wanted to understand poverty and hunger from the inside, not just by reading textbooks and listening to class lectures.

Indeed, there is no better way to grasp the truth than through lived experience. Can you really understand the pain of hunger if you have never gone hungry for a day? Is it possible for you to know what poverty is if you have never lacked anything? Roy and Dey took the unusually bold decision of renting a hut made of stone and mud in

Devdungri, located on National Highway 8 that connects Mumbai and Delhi. Giving up the comfort of the city, they began to live like their neighbours. They slept on the ground, went up to the well to draw water for their daily needs because there was no running tap, cooked roti and dal on a makeshift stove and washed their clothes and utensils themselves. A goat pen outside their hut was turned into a kitchen and bathing area, while the toilet was outside. As they embarked on their spartan new life, Roy and Dey were joined by Shankar Singh, a local man who, like them, was invested in working with the local community.

A gifted composer of songs, plays and puppet shows, Singh was a unique presence. He had a magnetic personality, he knew how to draw people in and mobilize them into action. When he realized his city-bred colleagues really wanted to help the villagers, he decided to help them build bridges with the locals, gain their trust and to explain to them the work they wanted to do in Devdungri. Without Singh's involvement, it would not have been possible for Roy and Dey to get as close to the people as they did—they may not have been able to break the barrier that separated educated, elite urban people like them from the poor, illiterate and mistrustful villagers.

Most of us who live in cities and suburban towns tend to associate villages with pastoral landscapes, lush green nature, cattle grazing, maybe a river gurgling by it. How many of you have drawn such a beautiful village scene when you were younger? But the real picture is far from pretty. Even in the twenty-first century, thousands of India's villages remain underdeveloped—many don't have access to clean drinking water, electricity and toilets.

Even worse are the prejudices that run through rural life. In many parts of the country, villages are still organized in terms of strict divisions of caste and labour. Those belonging to the so-called lower castes are expected to do menial labour, such as cleaning the garbage and human excreta. They are not allowed to draw water from the common well, denied entry into temples and barred from the homes of the 'upper castes'. Marriage between members of different castes is not only unacceptable, but it may even lead to revenge and bloodshed. Even ordinary practices, such as a lower-caste man growing a moustache or a lower-caste groom riding a horse to his wedding, has led the upper castes to rise in fury—beating, boycotting, sometimes murder have followed.

This is not to say that urban India is safer, superior or kinder than its rural counterpart.

MK Gandhi said India lives in its villages—which is true even in 2021. However, since 1947, people from the villages have been steadily moving to the cities in search of a better life. Forty years after independence, when Roy, Dey and Singh began to work in Devdungri, they realized it was the lack of adequate pay for the work they did that was forcing people to leave the village, apart from a desire to escape exploitation and injustice.

Three years after they started working together, Roy, Dey and Singh, along with a group of friends, supporters and well-wishers, founded the Majdoor Kisan Shakti Sangathan (MKSS) on 1 May 1990—also known as May Day, the day people around the world celebrate the working classes. MKSS soon helped shape a mass movement against deep-rooted corruption among the public servants who had been denying people their rightful wages and getting away with it for decades. In 1987, for instance, the minimum wage for a day's work was Rs 11. When MKSS began checking with people, they discovered some had been paid as little as Rs 2 per day, while most had got Rs 6—about half of the promised sum. No wonder people failed to make ends meet.

It was even less surprising that when MKSS approached the contractors, they got no satisfactory answers. Many flatly denied having cheated the workers, but also refused to show proof of paying them the full amount. A leader of the powerful Thakur caste lashed back furiously, threatening Dey and his associates with violence if they wouldn't stop meddling with affairs that didn't concern them. But the people had had enough. They weren't going to give up on their rightful demands now that they had the backing of MKSS.

Using street theatre that dramatized the suffering of the people, songs that celebrated the power of the collective and catchy slogans that demanded justice, MKSS began a campaign to raise public awareness, with Shankar Singh leading from the front. The mass meetings soon turned into hunger strikes—Roy was determined to follow the strategy of non-violent protest used by Gandhi during the freedom movement. After the first such public demonstration, the administration promised to compensate workers of their pending salaries. But their assurance turned out to be empty words. A new sit-in was organized at the nearby village of Bhim to put more pressure on the authorities. In spite of their meagre resources, villagers trooped in with food, money and grains—whatever they could afford to spare—to support those who sat on the dharna or strike.

The focus of the movement began to widen. While MKSS had started with lobbying for fair wages for workers, their demand soon graduated to requests for accessing the muster rolls, where all the payments were supposed to have been logged in. For the authorities, such a demand was unheard of, an outrageous insult to their sense of superiority. Desperately poor and unlettered, the villagers would have never imagined making such a request, let alone fight for it insistently. But now that the villagers had the support of the collective behind them, there was no looking back—even though they knew it was risky to provoke the fury of the officials and upper-caste leaders.

After months of sit-ins and hunger strikes, repeated threats from the upper castes and even failed attempts at bribing the protestors into giving up their demands, the muster rolls were finally read out to the public. As the meeting went on, waves of anger rippled through the crowd. Not only had they not been paid their dues, but the records were full of fudged numbers—expenses made to people who didn't exist, some who had been long dead, money had been even spent on buildings that did not exist and on projects that had never taken off!

The public auditing brought out in the open the extent of the corruption the villagers had been victims of. The so-called powerless people now began raising their voices, asking for 'accountability' of the 'accounts' that the administration had kept for so long. When Susheela, a woman who had studied only until Class IV, was questioned by journalists about her demands, she gave them a fitting answer. 'When I send my son to the market with Rs 10, I want accounts of how he has spent it once he's back home,' Susheela said. 'It's the same with the people and the government—they are sitting on our money, they must account for it to us.' You don't need big degrees or a fancy education to understand right from wrong: common sense is enough. Slowly, political parties began to take notice of MKSS and involve Roy in committees that would eventually help frame a law allowing people the right to know how the taxpayers' money was being spent.

India has a democratic system of governance—in fact, it is the world's largest democracy. This means it allows citizens who are eighteen or older to vote a government into power. It is logical, therefore, that people should also have the right to find out how the politicians they elect perform at their jobs. Are they fulfilling the promises they make in order to win their seat? Is the taxpayers' money being put to the right use—to improve the lives of the common people? Are political leaders investing in better education and hospitals? Are they creating more jobs so that everyone has a basic minimum income? How do they plan to deal with hunger and poverty? These questions concern us all, no matter who we are and whether we have had an education. It's not enough for the country's economy to grow—it must not harm the lives of the poor in the process. Forcibly taking away land from peasants and tribal people to build factories will not help end poverty. As Gandhi famously said, the world has enough for everyone's needs, but not for everyone's greed.

MKSS didn't simply stop at raising difficult questions— their next step was to ask for work for a fixed number of days every year so that people did not starve when the harvest was out of season. The right to work became as important as the right to information—both are meant to give every human being the means to live a life of basic dignity.

The first step towards achieving this goal, as Roy and Dey pointed out in a talk in 2010, was to stop looking at the poor as people who are 'different from us'. We, that is the educated urban elite who get to make policies and decisions, need to better understand the lives of the poor and their needs. It's a common mistake to imagine that the best way to deal with poverty is charity. The poor don't need our pity, they don't want to live off dole. Rather, they want to earn a living with dignity, by working hard like any self-respecting person and holding their heads high. MKSS members realized this truth early on in their field work in Devdungri.

After many setbacks faced by MKSS, in 2005 the Right to Information Act (RTI) came into effect, as did the National Rural Employment Guarantee Act or NREGA (it was later renamed the Mahatma Gandhi National Rural Employment Guarantee Act, or MGNREGA).

RTI allows Indian citizens the fundamental right to seek information from a public authority about almost anything—except for matters that are supposed to be official secrets. Since it came into effect, nearly 4500 RTI applications have been filed each day, a quarter of which are requests for information from the central government. Politicians and institutions in India clearly have a lot to answer to the people! In the first ten years since the RTI came into being, 17,500,000 petitions were filed. The rate has gone down since 2015, after the current central government came into power.

Although MKSS made history, the cost of their fight was enormous. As of 2018, more than 300 RTI activists have been attacked, physically threatened, mentally harassed, some even murdered, for exercising the power given to them by law. The powerful dislike being put under a scanner and will use every weapon in their arsenal to silence those who fight for truth and the right of the poor.

Even more worryingly, in 2019, a controversial change was made to the RTI law that gives the central government the power to decide how long the information commissioners—the officers who are supposed to make sure that people get the answers they are seeking—would be in office. Earlier, each officer served for a fixed term of five years. Their salaries, which were also fixed, are now determined by the government in power. When an authority gets the power to decide the duration of a person's job or how much money they would get paid, the person who they control is likely to do anything to keep them happy—including ignoring the law they are meant to uphold.

The story of RTI is still not over. And MKSS isn't giving up on their fight either.

THE FIGHT TO END THE WORST 'JOB' IN THE WORLD

Bezwada Wilson

b. 1966

How often have you noticed ragpickers walking with sacks filled with rubbish or rummaging in garbage dumps for scraps of plastic or paper and felt sad about the pitiful state of their lives? Horrific as their plight may be, believe it or not, there are people who are pushed into doing *even* worse work in order to earn a living.

It's likely that you live in a town or city, in an apartment or a house with toilets having running water. Most probably, you have never heard of 'dry latrines' and the disgusting practice of forcing a class of people to clean them every day. So, brace yourself for some ugly truths, for there's no other way of telling this story.

First, let's look at some facts and figures, without which we cannot even begin to understand the revolution that Bezwada Wilson, the hero of this chapter, has brought about in our country. According to the World Health Organization (WHO), as of 2019, some two billion people in the world live without access to basic sanitation. That means, among other things, they do not have access to proper toilets. In India, WHO estimates some 760 million people, mostly belonging to lower income groups in cities and villages, are forced to use 'dry latrines', or toilets without running water, to relieve themselves. And every morning a class of people is assigned to go from home to home to clean these dry latrines. These cleaners—most of them are women—are expected to do this appalling 'job', if you can think of it as one, without any mechanical equipment or protective gear. That's why they are usually called 'manual scavengers'. They use brooms and buckets to scoop out and collect human excreta with their bare hands, cover their faces with whatever cloth they can get so that they can block the stench, and then dump it all in a gutter some distance away. After cleaning dozens of such latrines, each of them gets a few hundred rupees at the end of the month.

The indignity of this 'profession' isn't all. The manual scavengers are usually not allowed to cross the threshold of the homes they service because of the 'unclean' nature of their work. Most dry latrines empty into chambers that can be accessed from outside a home. People on the streets avoid them if they know what they do for a living. Even shopkeepers are known to put their products on the ground when these cleaners come to buy groceries— because they do not want to touch them even by accident!

The worst part of the ordeal is the fact that these men and women are condemned to do this humiliating work over a lifetime, and are seldom given the option to free themselves from the clutches of such inhuman exploitation because of the evil of the caste system—if you are born into a family of manual scavengers, you are meant to carry on doing the same work through generations. Given the hazardous nature of their job, a great many of them develop painful diseases early on and don't live long— experts estimate the average lifespan of a manual scavenger to be forty to forty-five years. They end up spending their brief time on earth doing this menial task, with no hope of making something more of their lives or dreams.

As Wilson and his team found out, even in 2021, long after science and technology sent human beings to the moon, there are 770,000 Indians going into sewers to clean them every day, knowing full well the risk such work poses to their lives, while 2,600,000 community dry latrines continue to be used regularly all over the country. These numbers would have been far worse had it not been for the tireless efforts of one man and his colleagues.

Bezwada Wilson was born in 1966, to Bezwada Rachel and Bezwada Yacob, both of whom were manual scavengers, though they did not reveal the truth of their profession to their youngest child until many years later. The family lived in Kolar Gold Fields, on the border of Karnataka and Andhra Pradesh, so the Wilsons told their children that they worked in the gold mines, collecting ores. Wilson went to primary school in Andhra Pradesh and stayed at a hostel that was meant for students from scheduled castes and tribes. Later he went on to earn a BA degree in political science from B.R. Ambedkar University in Hyderabad. It was not until the 1980s that he came to have full knowledge of what his parents did to earn a living to take care of him and his siblings. And it was a series of accidents that led him to this harsh truth.

As a young man, Wilson kept seeing children from his lower-caste community dropping out of school. The parents failed to pay for their education because they barely managed to scrape together a living. And then, many of them ended up spending whatever little they earned on alcohol. Drinking numbed their senses, they told Wilson when he asked them about this vice; it helped them get through the terrible task of cleaning toilets that they were assigned to do every day. But when Wilson pressed for more information about why this work made them want to seek drink, these people wouldn't say more. Wracked by an intense feeling of shame, they simply clammed up. But addiction, which is a harmful and life-threatening habit, cannot be a solution to whatever it was that plagued them. So, Wilson decided to follow these people on the sly one morning, as they were setting out to work. What he found filled him with unspeakable horror.

As Wilson trailed them from home to home, he was aghast to see his neighbours handle human excreta and carry it far away to dispose of it. When one worker's bucket slipped into a dry pit of excreta, he put his hand in to pull it out. Shocked by this gesture, Wilson tried to stop the man, but was pushed aside and asked to leave him to do his work. Heartbroken by the scenes he witnessed, Wilson went home that day and told his parents of his experiences. It was only then that Rachel and Yacob revealed to their son that they, too, did the same work.

The knowledge shattered Wilson. He wept bitterly that day, even considered ending his life. But then, sense prevailed, and Wilson decided he would be better off staying alive and helping his community overcome the terrible predicament they had been thrust into. He wanted to end the practice of manual scavenging, but there were many hurdles before him, most of all from the very people who were doing this work.

As Wilson went around telling people of community they didn't have to accept their lot in life unquestioningly, he was met with panic and resistance. To begin with, his parents were not keen that Wilson, who they had taken the trouble of giving a decent education, should spend his time and energy on removing a practice that has existed for thousands of years.

The practice of gathering 'nightsoil', assigned to a class of 'slaves', was around in ancient Greece and Rome. In Asia, it persisted long after it had stopped in the West. In China and Japan, for example, the desperately poor were made to clean and transport human faeces, which was used as fertilizers in some parts.

Manual scavengers carried on with the work their ancestors had done, knowing no way of breaking the chain. Some even refused to admit that they did such work, or that it existed at all. The only way they could continue to live and carry on doing what they did was by choosing not to think of it actively, by remaining in a state of wilful denial.

After his graduation, Wilson went to the local Employment Exchange Office, only to be informed that he was fit for the one work that his parents have done all their lives. No matter how well he may have fared in college, Wilson was rudely told, he was only good enough to be a sanitation worker, since that was what people of his caste did. Insult was heaped on his already shaken mind, freshly reeling from the humiliation of discovering his family's occupation.

It was 1991 and India was preparing to mark the birth centenary of B.R. Ambedkar, the great Dalit leader, freedom fighter and architect of the country's Constitution. Twenty-five and smarting from the rejection he faced from society, Wilson began to read up on the man's ideas, which changed his life forever.

Like him, Ambedkar, too, had been born into a lower-caste family and fought hard to get the best education in the world, instead of meekly accepting the fate he was pushed into by birth. He broke barriers and travelled to New York and London to study at Columbia University and London School of Economics respectively. He established himself as an ace legal scholar and an economist of high repute.

DID YOU KNOW?

Ambedkar became a crusader for the rights of the low castes, especially the so-called untouchables, who, he said, were forced to become manual scavengers not because they were poor, weak and illiterate, but because society expected them to be nothing else. Their fight, Ambedkar told the Dalits, was not for wealth or power, 'it was the fight for reclamation of human dignity and personhood'.

The caste system in India, with its roots in the division of labour laid out since the Vedic times, was the evil that kept people bound to professions prescribed to them by the upper castes, and away from opportunities that would enable them to create a better life for themselves and their families. Ambedkar wrote several powerful books against the caste system but the one he is remembered for is *Annihilation of Caste*, which every Indian should read.

Inspired by Ambedkar's call, Wilson went to his people and urged them to join the Safai Karmachari Andolan (SKA), a movement led by manual scavengers to reclaim their right to live with dignity and bring about a social revolution.

The SKA, founded in 1993, was mostly restricted to Karnataka and Andhra Pradesh in the first decade of its existence, though the effect of the movement reached to other parts of the country, too. In 2003, Wilson, along with some of his colleagues, shifted base to New Delhi to create a national-level awareness of their mission. But in 1993, the year it took off, SKA got a big boost as Parliament enacted a law banning the construction of dry latrines and the practice of manual scavenging across India.

Passing a law, however, is only the first step towards bringing about change; the bigger challenge is to get people to think differently and discard their long-held prejudices. Even though dry latrines and manual scavenging were outlawed, both these practices continued as before—the custodians of the law, many of whom belonged to the upper castes, opted to look the other way. In fact, in Andhra Pradesh, activists working with SKA discovered dry latrines in a court complex of all places, which were being used by none other than the judges themselves! Enraged by such brazen hypocrisy, the SKA activists demolished the toilets.

Soon, thousands of manual scavengers and activists began to join SKA. Already, there was anger simmering among the lower castes for the disrespect they have been suffering for centuries; it needed only the slightest push for their resentment to erupt into a full-blown movement for social justice. Women manual scavengers staged their protest by burning the baskets they used to collect human excreta in. More dry latrines were pulled down. Along the way, Dalit activists like Paul Diwakar and IAS officer S.R. Sankaran lent their support, as did thousands of volunteers, who went around states, on 'Bhim Yatras' by buses, making a note of every dry latrine and manual scavenger they could find. After a decade of mobilizing the workers and meticulously recording every violation of the law, the SKA went to the Supreme Court with a list of all the departments of government—such as the railways, education, defence and judiciary—that were still employing manual scavengers in violation of the law. Some two dozen hearings followed, several people were taken into custody, but the practice of manual scavenging did not stop still.

In 2007, Wilson and his SKA colleagues went a step further. It wasn't enough, they decided, to merely demand an end to manual scavenging—they would have to find new employment opportunities for the workers to help them leave their work and make a fresh start. The idea made sense, but getting it moving wasn't easy. Governments assume that their responsibility towards the poor and marginalized people begins and ends with giving them money to start a business or buy cattle so that they can focus on farming. But imagine what you would do if you were suddenly given an aeroplane one day and asked to fly people around the world.

The manual scavengers, most of whom were barely literate if at all, were caught in a similar situation. It was not enough to give them the means to start a business. They would have to be trained on how to launch it, manage it on a day-to-day basis, sustain it and make it grow. How would a person with no experience of ever running a shop and without any formal education do all this? Worse still, if their caste became known, their stores may be boycotted by others and land them in even bigger trouble.

In 2013, yet another law was passed to tighten the ban on manual scavenging. Among other areas, it focused on finding alternative professions for people through a systematic survey. SKA volunteers began to speak to manual scavengers to understand their needs and training them to develop their interests. Eventually, women who once spent each day cleaning latrines found their feet by launching small ventures: one started selling clothes, another driving a scooter to transport people around her city, yet another opened a shop selling cosmetic products. The move to build toilets with flushes and running water, in public as well as private homes, began to gain steam around the country. Again, Wilson was a step ahead in thinking through this shift. It wasn't enough to build bathrooms, he said, the government as well as the public should also figure out a way of keeping these places clean so that the responsibility was not foisted on only one section of society who have done such degrading labour through generations.

In 2016, as Wilson turned fifty, he was chosen for the prestigious Ramon Magsaysay Award, given annually in memory of the former Philippine president to people who have made a mark through their outstanding service to society. Wilson dedicated this honour to everyone who was part of the SKA and had joined the fight to defeat oppression, especially the brave women who gave up their inhuman work and rose in protest. Even though Wilson and his comrades have come a long way and achieved historic results, manual scavenging is far from erased in India. So, the next time you use a public toilet, do spare a thought for the person whose job is to keep it spick and span—and also for the thousands of others you don't see, who still start their day by cleaning other people's excreta. Then say a quick thanks to heroes like Wilson, who are fighting every day to bring dignity and respect to such invisible labour.

A RIVER AND ITS PEOPLE

Medha Patkar and the Narmada Bachao Andolan

b. 1954

India is a nation of many rivers, which support millions of lives that bloom and sprout on their banks—cities and towns, people and plants, animals and industries. But like every natural resource, be it forests or mineral ores, rivers are also much in demand. Powerful businesses and governments want to build dams that would tame rivers to generate electricity, direct their courses to specific regions to help farmers irrigate their land and supply cities with their daily water needs. On the face of it, these intentions sound reasonable. Why shouldn't we work together with nature to improve our lives, take care of our cities and factories? But the problem arises when we jump into such projects with a selfish mindset, without paying any attention to what people who have lived off rivers for decades have to say about our plans, or without considering the ecological cost of our ambitions.

It was this clash between the desire to harness the might of nature and the interests of people who are nurtured by it that gave rise to the longest Gandhian movement in modern India, the Narmada Bachao Andolan. And the name of one woman who steered it from the start shines bright to this day, known as much in India as across the world.

Medha Patkar was born in 1954 to parents who led politically and socially active lives. Her father, Vasant Khanolkar, had been part of the freedom struggle and later fought for the rights of workers, while her mother, Indumati, who was a government officer, ran a women's organization. In the 1950s, India was a young republic, excited about the promise of development and prosperity. The first prime minister of the nation, Jawaharlal Nehru, was a leader with foresight, who supported science, technology and modernization. In 1955, when Patkar was a toddler, Nehru declared dams to be the 'temples of modern India'. Little did he know at the time that his statement would become a touchstone for generations of leaders, who would use (rather, misuse) it to justify their greed. But even less known is the fact that Nehru, the visionary leader that he was, realized the folly of his words soon enough. As Patkar pointed out in an interview in 2004, in 1958, Nehru revised his blind faith in large dams by describing them as 'the disease of gigantism that we must withdraw from'. Sadly, only the first part of his views is common knowledge; we have chosen to overlook the rest.

The trouble started when Gujarat, Madhya Pradesh and Maharashtra, the states through which Narmada River flows, got involved in a dispute over sharing its waters. A proposal was drawn up to build a series of big and small dams across the river to control its course so that the three states could use its water to meet their different needs.

While Gujarat was in favour of the proposal, Madhya Pradesh and Maharashtra were opposed, as were the adivasis, farmers, environmental scientists and human rights activists, who sensed the danger that lurked in such a plan. Dams, people argued, would lead to water logging in the region, leading to devastating floods that would damage thousands of homes and destroy acres of land meant for agriculture. The soil around the area could also lose its fertility, leading to a failure of crops. But the supporters of dams countered with their own logic: the long-term gains of building these dams would outweigh the suffering of a few people, they argued. The success of such projects will not only lead to better supply of water to cities and help generate electricity but also create many new jobs, they said.

The damage caused by large dams in India is difficult to measure since the victims of such projects are usually the very poor people, who live in rural areas, the adivasis and Dalits, who barely register on the radar of the state. They wait for the land they have lost to be returned to them for generations, as is the case, for example, with those who were displaced by the Pong Dam in Kangra, Himachal Pradesh, some fifty years ago. Till date, some 8000 families have not even *seen* the land that was promised to them in return.

So what good is development that comes at the cost of causing harm to some so that others may benefit from it? This question continues to haunt India, as industries come up around the country, factories spew toxic smoke into the air, causing health hazards to humans and release sludge into the rivers, killing fish and other marine lives. You may have read about elephants being hit by trains that run at high speed through forested areas. In cities, hundreds of trees are cut down to build highways, while national parks and tiger reserves are being invaded for coal and sand mining.

In 1969, the Narmada Water Disputes Tribunal was set up to weigh the pros and cons of building the dams along the river. It took ten years for the tribunal to come to a decision. In 1979, permission was granted to start work and the Sardar Sarovar Dam, the biggest among the dams whose foundation stone had been laid by Nehru in 1961, finally took off. But by 1985, the project had ground to a temporary halt, as the Ministry of Environment found out that the environmental clearances that were required before starting the project had not been approved.

Around this time Patkar, a doctoral student of social work at the Tata Institute of Social Sciences in Mumbai, arrived on the scene along with her supporters. To their shock, they discovered that the poor villagers who were going to lose their homes to the dams had not even been consulted before the decision was taken to go ahead with the project. While they were told by the authorities that they would be resettled, there was no proper plan or a timeline to do so. Yet, a few months later in 1986, the governments of Gujarat, Karnataka and Madhya Pradesh approached the World Bank to finance the project. The plan was to build thirty major, 135 medium and 3000 small dams along Narmada River—it could cause immense suffering to thousands, if not done with extreme caution.

Patkar and her supporters were outraged by the sheer disregard for public opinion, especially of those who would pay a heavy price, with their lives no less, to fulfil the interest of others. It was not that she and her team were opposed to the very idea of development. But they objected to the way in which it was being brought about.

'Rights should be granted to the smallest unit of population,' as Patkar said in an interview, 'and the benefits should first take care of that unit, moving upward.' In other words, we have to first respect the rights of the people who live in the region through which the Narmada flows, seek their views on the dam-building project, before we proceed with it.

How would you feel if the government came and demolished the building you live in one day because it wished to build a new highway through your neighbourhood? Even if you were assured you would be moved with your family into a new home, you may still never want to see the house you grew up in turned into rubble! Imagine the pain the villagers felt when they saw their homes, where they had lived for generations, being washed away by roaring floods, simply because a group of people more powerful than them had decided that big dams were a good idea!

To stop this injustice against the poor villagers, the Narmada Bachao Andolan (Save the Narmada Movement) was launched under the leadership of Patkar. In 1986, as the World Bank decided to finance the building of the dams along the river, Patkar and her followers took out a thirty-six-day march across the states through which the river flows. The protestors decided to follow in the footsteps of MK Gandhi and demonstrate peacefully. They folded their hands to indicate they did not mean any harm, some even tied their hands in a show of non-violence, as they walked along. Their strategy, however, did not protect them from attacks by the police as they reached the border of Gujarat. There, Patkar said later, the marchers were caned, arrested and the clothes of the women in the group were torn off by the keepers of law and order. This was only the start of a long struggle to provide the residents of the Narmada valley access to crucial information and legal help to deal with the impact of the project that was already well underway. Patkar and her followers would go on to make many more dramatic gestures of protest. Several times, they stood in the river as the water level rose up to their waists—even up to Patkar's neck once—until they had to be forcibly removed by the police.

In the course of their investigations, Patkar and the Narmada Bachao Andolan found, to their shock, that the World Bank was aware of the damage to the environment that the dams would cause. After repeated dharnas and highlighting of these problems in the international press by activists, the World Bank decided to withdraw from it in 1993. But the triumph was short-lived, as the Indian government stepped in with additional funding for the project. In 1995, another temporary victory came the way of the Narmada Bachao Andolan after the Supreme Court heeded its appeal and stopped the construction of the Sardar Sarovar Dam until the government had created a plan that did not violate environmental regulations or harmed the lives of the people in the valley. Yet again, it proved to be only a temporary relief, as the same court allowed the work on the dam to resume in 1999.

In spite of this see-saw of ups and downs, Patkar and her followers were firm in their resolve to make the world notice the tragedy that had befallen a small community in India. In 1999, she travelled to Seattle, with some of her colleagues to protest against the World Trade Organization (WTO). The WTO, they argued, followed a one-size-fits-all model of making policies—that is to say, the WTO's plan to help the poor in Africa cannot be applied without modifications to solve the problems of poverty in Asia.

In 2000, Patkar was back again on the streets with her colleagues, this time in Prague, to raise slogans against the way large corporations like the International Monetary Fund and the World Bank worked against the interests of the vulnerable.

In India, too, people from different walks of life were gradually being drawn to Patkar's indomitable spirit, her ability to go on long fasts, as Gandhi also did (one fast by Patkar lasted more than three weeks and nearly ended her life), to fight for the right of the poor to live with dignity. In 1990, during the early days of the movement, social worker and activist Baba Amte, who is best remembered for helping improve the lives of people suffering from the stigma of leprosy, moved to the Narmada valley to work with Patkar. In the late 1990s, writer Arundhati Roy, who had created an international buzz after winning the prestigious Booker Prize in 1997 for her novel *The God of Small Things*, offered her support too. She was even detained in a jail for one day in 2002 after she criticized the Supreme Court's decision to allow work on the dams to continue, even as thousands of lives were lost due to flooding or suicide, an extreme step desperate farmers were taking recourse to.

The legal battles raged on for years. In 2011, for instance, the Supreme Court even observed that Narmada Bachao Andolan had provided false information under oath, an extremely serious offence. Through thick and thin, Patkar and the Narmada Bachao Andolan kept fighting for the rights of the people of the valley, even as work on the dams continued. By 2006, the height of the Sardar Sarovar Dam had been raised several times—it was 400 feet tall, from its original 260 feet. In 2017, soon after Prime

Minister Narendra Modi formally inaugurated it, its height
was further raised to nearly 535 feet, double its initial size!

The story of Narmada Bachao Andolan isn't over yet,
nor is Patkar's fight for justice. In the last two decades,
alongside her work in Narmada valley, she launched
several prominent movements, such as the Ghar Bachao
Ghar Banao Andolan in 2015, to fight for housing rights
of the poor when the government of Maharashtra decided
to demolish 75,000 homes in Mumbai. The year before,
in 2004, Patkar started a political party called People's
Political Front, along with members of the National
Alliance of People's Movement, a collective of activists and
social workers she had formed earlier. In spite of mounting
pressure to stand in elections, Patkar stayed away from
active politics for a long time, choosing to focus instead
on raising political awareness among the people. In 2007,
she was in the news again, as she spoke up against Tata
Motors, which was on its way to build the Nano small-
car factory in Singur, West Bengal by taking away 997
acres of agricultural land from farmers. The following
year, she joined poor villagers of Nandigram to fight off
another attempt to grab farmland by the government of
West Bengal, this time to set up industries and a special
economic zone.

In recent times, Patkar tried to make a start in politics,
when she joined the Aam Aadmi Party in 2014, but lost
the North East Mumbai constituency in the Lok Sabha
elections that year. She resigned from the party in 2015
and returned to her work as a grassroots activist. Since
then, she has taken up cudgels on behalf of a teenage Dalit
girl in Hathras, Uttar Pradesh, who was gangraped and
murdered in 2020. Later that year, when the farmers of

India erupted in protests against new laws that would harm their interests, she again offered her support. 'The farmers are fighting to strengthen democracy in India, and this will help the oppressed people to raise their voices,' she told journalists as she sat with a group of protesters in Shahjahanpur in Uttar Pradesh in 2021. In that one sentence, Patkar summed up her life's mission too—to help those who fall through the cracks of the government's plans find their voice. That's precisely what she set out to do with the Narmada Bachao Andolan—and it is a vision she remains faithful to.

The Narmada Bachao Andolan may not have been able to stop the construction of large dams or the displacement of thousands, but it has taken their stories to the world. It has allowed them a chance to express their opinion in matters that concern not only the development of the nation but also their lives and deaths.

THE HEALER OF DAMAGED HEARTS

Dr Devi Shetty
b. 1953

How many of you wanted to be a doctor when you were little? Maybe some of you still do when you grow up. As small children, did you have a miniature doctors' set, with a plastic stethoscope, tiny scalpels, pill boxes and cotton wool to play with? Many of us are fascinated by surgery when we are young. The idea that broken bones and unwell organs can be fixed by cutting open the body, then sewing it back together with thread and needle almost sounds like something out of a fairy tale.

But beyond fairy tales, in the real world we live in, there are surgeons who have the incredible gift of putting us to sleep, opening our bodies, mending any flaws inside it, then stitching it back together before waking us up from our slumber. And most of the time, lo and behold, our bodies bounce back to robust health; such is the miracle of modern medicine. Dr Devi Shetty is one such healer, specializing in repairing damaged hearts and treating ones that are ill. His knowledge is vast and skill exceptional, especially as a surgeon who operates on babies as young as a few days old. The heart of an infant that age is about the size of a walnut, or even smaller, so you can imagine the care and confidence a surgeon needs to have in order to operate on such a tiny and delicate organ!

Thousands of babies in India are born with defective hearts every year, which can give rise to serious health conditions, from breathing trouble to their little bodies turning blue due to lack of oxygen in the bloodstream. In most cases where a baby is born with one or more holes in its heart, the condition is treatable, but needs to be addressed swiftly. Any delay can cause lasting damage to the baby's systems and, in the worst-case scenario, death. But medical treatment of this nature is usually prohibitively expensive for most people, especially in a country like ours, families can seldom afford to shell out a huge sum of money at short notice.

Apart from being a surgeon with rare abilities, Dr Shetty also found a solution to cutting down the costs of heart surgeries, including the possibility of treating thousands of children and adults free of cost. Indeed, he has proved to the world that in order to be a good doctor, it is not enough to acquire knowledge from years of study and hands-on practice. A visionary physician like Dr Shetty is someone with immense compassion, aware of the hardships of the people around him and born with a unique fighting spirit, one that pushes him to seek solutions when faced with hardships, instead of meekly surrendering himself to fate. A deeply committed doctor is someone who has his heart in the right place, before he undertakes to heal the ailing hearts of others.

Dr Shetty was born in 1953 in the Dakshina Kannada district of Karnataka, the eighth of nine children. By the time he was a young boy, his parents were already middle-aged, not keeping well and frequently in and out of hospitals. His childhood was spent in fear of losing his mother to disease, Dr Shetty told an interviewer many years later. Yet, even at a young age, he was aware of someone called a 'doctor', who had the amazing power to heal his mother and keep her alive. And so, early on, he decided to become a doctor himself when he grew up.

There was another big factor behind this ambition. In 1967, while he was still a school student, Dr Shetty heard of a world-famous doctor called Christian Barnard, a South African who had, for the first time, performed a human-to-human heart transplant. In an unheard-of feat of daring, Dr Barnard took out the heart of an accident victim and put it into the chest of a fifty-four-year-old man. Although the recipient died of complications brought on by pneumonia eighteen days after the surgery, the successful transplant procedure was a landmark in the history of medicine, word of which spread around the globe and reached the ears of a young boy in India. Inspired, Dr Shetty set on his career path, by first becoming a medical student in India, followed by a stint at Guy's Hospital in London, where he had the experience of operating on patients.

From the very beginning, Dr Shetty had incredible stamina, the capacity to work for long hours without a break. At Guy's, he took on weekend duties and signed up to perform as many surgeries as he could, sometimes without checking with his supervisor first. Although he was initially scolded for exceeding his call of duty, the senior doctors soon discovered he was unusually talented and stopped objecting to these indiscretions.

In 1989, Dr Shetty returned to India after spending several years in the UK, armed with the FRCS, or Fellowship of the Royal Colleges of Surgeons, qualification, which allowed him to practice as a senior surgeon in Ireland or the UK. He could have easily settled abroad and had a flourishing career there, but he had made a pledge to himself to help the millions in his country who were suffering from, or dying of, heart diseases. So he joined the BM Birla hospital in Kolkata as a cardiac surgeon (cardiac is the medical term for anything related to the heart). Soon after, Dr Shetty made a splash by performing India's first neonatal surgery, which, in plain English, means surgery on a newborn baby. His patient was nine days old. The entire nation was awestruck by Dr Shetty's daring and technical mastery, most of all his calm confidence.

Since then, Dr Shetty has performed over 15,000 heart surgeries in India. His patients have included many thousand babies and young children as well as celebrities. Even though he is based in Bengaluru, he is often called upon to consult on the cardiac health of famous people. You may have read in the news recently that when Sourav Ganguly, former Indian cricket skipper and current president of the Board of Control for Cricket in India, had a heart attack, Dr Shetty flew down to Kolkata to check on his health and the progress of his treatment. In the 1990s, while he was still working in Kolkata, Dr Shetty had to attend to another celebrity, who ended up changing his life and his outlook on medicine altogether.

One day, Dr Shetty's office received a call requesting a home visit, which was odd, because surgeons do not take on such duties. But the caller was insistent. If he made an exception this one time, they insisted, the visit might end up changing Dr Shetty's own life forever. Curious, Dr Shetty decided to head over to the address he was given. As he reached his destination, he realized he was at the Missionaries of Charity, founded by none other than Mother Teresa. His patient, in fact, was the nun and social worker herself, now canonized as Saint Teresa.

At the time, Mother Teresa was in her eighties and her health was fragile, especially her heart, which had been suffering for several years. Dr Shetty decided to take on Mother Teresa as his patient, operated on her heart and cared for her for the last years of her life. Spending time around Mother Teresa, Dr Shetty has said, as have many others close to her, was like being in the presence of the divine. During her stays at the hospital, when Mother would be better enough to walk around, she would often join Dr Shetty in his daily rounds, meeting his patients along with him. She was especially struck by the love and care with which Dr Shetty looked after his little patients in the children's ward. Dr Shetty remembered one day, as they were both walking from bed to bed, when Mother Teresa turned to him and said, 'I know why you are here, Dr Shetty . . . When God created these little children with defective hearts, He realized there was a problem and that's the reason why He sent you to fix them.' It was the best definition of a cardiac surgeon, Dr Shetty admitted, he had ever heard in his life.

Mother Teresa's selfless service towards the poorest of the poor had a profound effect on Dr Shetty's life and career. Soon after, he left Kolkata and returned to Bengaluru, where, in 2001, he founded Narayana Hrudayalaya, a state-of-the-art heart hospital that would not turn away any patient just because they did not have the ability to pay for their treatment. The idea was revolutionary because it was not charity that Dr Shetty was interested in; on the contrary, he had a deeply-thought-out plan of action that would also enable him to run his hospital as a sustainable business.

The cost of private healthcare, Dr Shetty argued, would become significantly lesser if hospitals adopted the concept of 'economies of scale'. In other words, if an institution can treat more people in less time without compromising on the quality of treatment, then the sheer numbers would help bring down the costs involved. That would be a win-win situation for both doctors and patients. At Narayana Hrudayalaya, for instance, there are some 1000 beds, with a team of doctors conducting thirty major surgeries daily and attending to 15,000 people at the outpatient department every day. These high numbers, along with swift admission, diagnosis, operation, recovery and release from the hospital, as opposed to spending days clocking up high bills in other private hospitals, bring down the cost of treatment significantly. So much that those who cannot afford to pay anything at all are not refused care at Narayana Hrudayalaya—the cost of their treatment is written off by the money that is paid by those who can for their surgeries.

One of Dr Shetty's missions in life is to separate access to good healthcare from affluence, the social status of a person or the amount of wealth they possess. 'Like we get oxygen, air and water, healthcare should become available to everyone on this planet naturally. And that can be done,' he says in the Netflix documentary series *The Surgeon's Cut*. On the premises of Narayana Hrudayalaya are a temple, a mosque, a gurdwara and a chapel, welcoming people from all faiths with the promise of being treated with respect, dignity and care. Patients are bussed in from different parts of the state so that lack of access to transport does not get in their way of receiving the best treatment.

Dr Shetty is especially passionate about the belief that babies should not be born into this world with a price tag attached to their lives. At his hospital, 60 per cent of the patients pay very little for the treatment they get, and no one is ever turned away for not having enough money. When it comes to treating young babies, the staff at Narayana Hrudayalaya are trained to be especially sensitive to the family's needs, but also aware of the biases that run in Indian society, where people are more likely to go that extra mile to raise money for the treatment of baby boys. So, the doctors there assume a softer and kinder approach towards parents of baby girls.

It is typical of Dr Shetty to be so keenly aware of social realities and train his colleagues to hone such instincts. As a young physician, for instance, he realized that even if he had successfully operated on patients and cured their ailing hearts, many, especially the poorest of them, took a long time to recover, and often failed to do so, because their bodies lacked basic nourishment. So Dr Shetty started bringing eggs cooked from his home and began to distribute them among poor and malnourished patients so that their bodies would get a regular supply of protein and heal faster. No wonder there came a time when he was nicknamed 'The Egg Doctor' by his patients!

When it came to training young surgeons, Dr Shetty followed an unconventional path, too. Trainees at Narayana

Hrudayalaya, which is a teaching hospital, are expected to attend painting classes to learn to handle the instruments with which they operate as delicately as paintbrushes. Dr Shetty believes that such unusual experiences change the doctors' entire perspective on surgery. 'Ultimately [surgeons] are all artists, creating masterpieces,' he once said in an interview. 'Whatever we do should look beautiful in the end. If it looks beautiful, it always works.'

Every year, two million people in our country need to have heart surgeries, but only 1,50,000 procedures are performed. The difference in numbers is not only due to the lack of facilities or funds, but also because people aren't even aware that they need cardiac care because they are too poor to visit a doctor for a health check-up.

A heart transplant in a private hospital in India (very few of these have the facility to do such a surgery anyway) can easily cost Rs 20-25 lakhs—whereas the average family income of some of the poorest patients Dr Shetty treats at Narayana Hrudayalaya is a few thousand rupees a month!

What Dr Shetty has done for affordable healthcare in India is undoubtedly unique, but we need many more like him, who are willing to pledge their energies to making the world a better place for all. Perhaps keeping this need in mind, Dr Shetty wrote a moving letter on reaching a personal as well as professional landmark. After the 4000th surgery he performed on children without charging a fee, he addressed these former patients of his, some of whom were now full-grown healthy adults, explaining to them the reason behind his decision to treat them for free.

The tragedy of their being born with a faulty heart in a poor 'third world' country was to have 'a price tag' attached to their lives when they were just ten days old, Dr Shetty wrote. 'If your parents paid the price, they could have you; if not, you would have to go back to where you came from.' But then, they came to him for help and were not disappointed. At the end of this beautiful letter, which you can find on the internet, Dr Shetty made one request of these 4000 children: 'All I ask you for is: Can you spare a few moments of your precious time every day for someone who needs it? And that, too, without expecting anything back in return. Do you know, to save your life, a few hundred people worked sincerely without expecting any remuneration other than the joy of making your family, friends and relatives happy?' he wrote.

'Dear children, we are all creations of God, and He is in control of all the events happening in this world. Unfortunately, He is not supposed to be seen, heard or felt. So, He runs this world using people like you and me. And when you do your work without expecting anything in return, just for the joy of bringing happiness to others, that's when you'll realize it is not your hands which do the job, it is the hands of God.'

For each of us, the meaning of God is deeply private and different; our lives may or may not have been touched by the gift of Dr Shetty's healing hands, but we can always believe in the magical power of his message and try to live by it as fully as we can.

THE FIGHT FOR SAFE WORKPLACES

Bhanwari Devi

It is likely that you have come across the term 'MeToo' already. Since 2018, it has regularly appeared on television debates, the internet, in newspapers and magazines across India. You may have heard people speak of it. You probably know that it refers to a movement that first took off on social media, where women from different parts of the world joined voices to speak up against injustices they have faced—and are still facing—at the workplace from their male colleagues and bosses.

None of this is news—at least to most women. But suddenly, the scale of the problem was laid bare for everyone to see.

For centuries, women around the world have mostly suffered in silence at the hands of men—at home, work or on the streets. Even those who refused to stay quiet usually had little hope of getting a fair hearing from the law. In many countries, including India, the burden of proving such crimes was largely put on the already suffering women, adding insult to injury. It was no different when the MeToo movement broke out. The accusations were mostly greeted with naïve disbelief or mounting outrage.

But thirty years ago, it was due to the bravery of one unlettered village woman that India witnessed its first MeToo moment—long before there was any internet or social media, let alone the name we now know this movement by.

In 1992, Bhanwari Devi was just another twenty-five-year-old woman from the kumhar community (who are potters by profession) living in a village in Rajasthan, near the state's capital, Jaipur. But in many ways she was unlike the women around her. When the state government launched a campaign to stop people from getting their children married off before they came of age, Bhanwari Devi volunteered to act as a saathin—a woman whose job was to spread awareness about the evils of child marriage.

The challenge was truly monumental. It was a long-established custom in the rural parts of Rajasthan to get children married when they were barely a few years (sometimes months!) old, long before they were anywhere near the legal age of marriage—eighteen for girls and twenty-one for boys. Local sentiments were so strong about this tradition that the police found it difficult to intervene. Even if they succeeded in stopping a wedding, the parents often found another opportunity within days to get the deed done. It was clear that the fear of the law alone wasn't going to put an end to this nasty practice.

So women like Bhanwari Devi, who were familiar with the locals and their beliefs, were trained to go around and explain to them the importance of waiting to get their children married until they attained the legal age. Poor, illiterate and from a lower caste, Bhanwari Devi was a victim of this horrible custom herself, married off when she was a baby. At an age when she should have looked forward to playing with other children and going to school, she was dressed up as a bride and forced to step into an adult world. That's why she took it upon herself to stop the practice with such conviction.

Soon after becoming a saathin, Bhanwari Devi discovered that two children—one of them only nine months old—were about to be married off to each other by their parents in her village. She wasted no time in trying to prevent it, reasoning with the families to call off the wedding. But instead of listening to her, the parents were enraged. The father of the infant bride, who belonged to the powerful Gujar caste, persuaded the entire village to boycott Bhanwari Devi and her husband Mohan Lal as punishment for meddling in their private affairs and calling the police. Out of fear of the Gujars, most people stopped doing business with the couple. The fields they cultivated were destroyed.

But the revenge did not end there.

Days later, five men from the Gujar caste, including the man whose daughter's wedding Bhanwari Devi had tried to stop, cornered her and her husband while they were out, working. First, they started beating up Mohan Lal and then, as Bhanwari Devi tried to stop them, a couple of them pinned her to the ground. Then, one by one, the men took turns to rape her. The message was loud and clear—and brutally delivered.

Although bruised and battered, Bhanwari Devi refused to retreat meekly back into the shadows. Instead, she decided to lodge a complaint with the police, a rare act of courage for people of her caste, let alone women of her community, who are taught, from the day they are born, to steel themselves against every indignity inflicted upon them by society. Not surprisingly, the police were not willing to register a report. But Bhanwari Devi and her co-worker, who had gone to the station with her, refused to give up until their demand was met. At last, after the department of women and child development, for which Bhanwari Devi was working as a volunteer, spoke up on her behalf, the police sat up. But still, matters did not improve much.

Bhanwari Devi had to wait for almost two days before she was examined by a medical doctor. When she finally thought her ordeal was over, she was asked to take off her lehenga and hand it over for the investigation. Mohan Lal removed his turban so that Bhanwari Devi could wrap it around herself and return home.

DID YOU KNOW?

- The law currently says that a woman should be medically examined within twenty-four hours of lodging a complaint of rape with the police.

- If the doctor conducting the test is male, there should be a female attendant present in the room. No one else should be around other than these two persons.

- The woman should not be harassed while registering the complaint. The police should also arrange for a counsellor to attend to the stress and mental suffering she is going through.

At long last, when the matter went to court, the judges refused to believe that upper-caste men would lay their hands on a lower-caste woman—because, according to the ancient rules of caste purity, behaving in such a manner would amount to defiling themselves. It was a shockingly insensitive conclusion. As though her indignity in court was not enough, most of Bhanwari Devi's neighbours were critical of her decision to fight for justice. They accused her of lying about the attack and continued to shun Mohan Lal and her. The few who wanted to support her could not come out in the open, afraid of upsetting the Gujars.

But Bhanwari Devi had caught the attention of several women's rights groups, who listened to her, advised her and made sure her tremendous act of courage did not go to waste. And so, even though the justice system failed Bhanwari Devi, she became an icon of the women's rights movement all over India. Since she was attacked while she was doing her work, a women's collective called Vishaka went to the Supreme Court asking for a set of rules and regulations to be framed that would protect Indian women at their workplaces. And thus, one bold step taken by an illiterate villager became a giant stride for all women, and the Vishaka guidelines were drafted in 1997.

HIGHLIGHTS OF THE VISHAKA GUIDELINES

- Both employers and employees should clearly understand what counts as harassment

- Employers should create a safe working environment for employees to express themselves without any fear.

Information about the process of filing complaints should be available on the company's website and posted in other parts of the office.

- Every workplace should have an Internal Complaints Committee, or ICC, which should investigate any complaint as speedily as possible and file its report. The offender must be punished and the complainant given a compensation if the charges are proved.

While the Vishaka guidelines led to a law to safeguard the rights of working women in 2013, doubts remained about its reach on the ground. It's one thing to make promises on paper, but that doesn't necessarily give women the power to take on mighty villains. Five more years went by, until another landmark case proved that women could, indeed, speak up against men who have misbehaved with them and hope to get a patient hearing from the courts.

Around 2018, the MeToo movement, which had started in the US, reached India well and truly. That year, former Miss India and actor Tanushree Dutta complained that Nana Patekar, her co-star in the 2008 movie *Horn Ok Pleassss*, had behaved inappropriately with her on the sets, while they were filming a song. Even though she had registered her protest at the time, no action was taken either by the film's crew or the police. On the contrary, Dutta was heckled by Patekar's supporters, forced to retreat from the scene of crime with her head hung in shame. But ten years later, the mood was different. With the MeToo movement gaining momentum, the world was forced to pay closer attention to the complaints that were being publicly aired by women on social media platforms.

In the US, MeToo exposed a famous Hollywood movie producer called Harvey Weinstein for harassing scores of women who had worked with him over the years. His behaviour ranged from violent physical attacks to mental torture. When some of these women, mostly young and inexperienced, tried to speak up against him, they were shushed by Weinstein's team of lawyers and threatened with lawsuits they did not have the means to fight. Taking on such a powerful opponent, these women were made to understand, would bring an end to their career in the movie industry. So, Weinstein's abuse went on unchecked— until the silence ended in 2017.

Since then, following investigations by journalists like Jodi Kantor, Megan Twohey and Ronan Farrow, scores of women have come forward to accuse Weinstein of misbehaving with them—including superstars like Gwyneth Paltrow, Cate Blanchett and Helena Bonham Carter. A New York court found him guilty on several counts in 2020, and finally sent him to jail to serve a sentence for twenty-three years. It is certainly a start, and a big one too, but there are hundreds of Weinsteins living among us who are yet to get their comeuppance.

Taking cue from the Weinstein incident, an Indian scholar called Raya Sarkar, living in the USA, prepared a list of names of university and college professors who were known to behave improperly with their students. Their actions were open secrets, though no one could do much about their conduct. So Sarkar hoped to end this culture of silence and send out a warning to young women against such horrible teachers. Before long, dozens of women began to come forward with personal stories of suffering at the hands of some of these men—and many others. The pattern was almost identical in every case. Even where they had complained, the system failed the women.

It is often hard to believe someone you know well could behave badly with a woman. But that is as absurd as claiming that since you have not seen your best friend cheat in an exam, no one else could have caught them in the act either. The rule of thumb is to believe the victim instead of blaming them. They have suffered enough already.

You might also wonder why, instead of naming and shaming the culprits, the victims were not taking them to the law. Sadly, in India, not only are the courts bogged down with piles of unresolved cases but complaining against the rich and powerful is also never an obvious choice. For one, there are huge expenses involved in fighting a case. And second, even if a woman were to complain to her employers against her boss, it is unlikely that the person in the position of power would face any consequences.

Around this time, journalist Priya Ramani spoke up about suffering at the hands of an unnamed senior male journalist years ago. As a young aspiring reporter, she had gone to meet him for a job interview at a hotel he was staying in Mumbai. Instead of meeting her at the lobby, which is a suitable venue for a professional interview, the man insisted she come up to his room. Once she was there, he asked her a series of uncomfortable questions, made improper suggestions and generally behaved in a way that made her nervous and afraid for her safety. Somehow

Ramani managed to run away from him at the end of the disturbing meeting.

Years later, when she wrote her story in a magazine, it took some quick guesswork to put two and two together. Soon it became well-known that the accused was none other than former journalist and editor MJ Akbar, who was, at the time, a politician and minister with the ruling BJP government. In the days that followed, dozens of women came out on social media with their personal accounts of suffering at his hands when they were young journalists. It was India's Weinstein moment—in more senses than one.

For, rather like Weinstein, Akbar decided to take Ramani to court. He accused her of destroying his reputation and public standing. The trial went on for nearly two years, with lawyers on both sides leaving no stone unturned to defend their clients. Ramani, who lives in Bengaluru, flew down to Delhi for the hearings, stuck to her stand and, despite a barrage of hard-hitting questions thrown at her by Akbar's lawyers, answered them calmly. She was confident that the truth was going to prevail at the end of the day.

And it did!

After months of suspense, the court came to the conclusion that Ramani could not be accused of defaming Akbar because he 'was not a man of stellar reputation' in the first place. The judge also defended a woman's right to express her grievance on any platform, though decades may have passed between the incident and her complaint, as was the case with Ramani and Akbar. The pain and shame associated with such incidents are such that it may take a long time for the victim to be able to speak about it to others. Some may not be able to do that all their lives.

Like Bhanwari Devi, Ramani created a platform for Indian women to demand to be treated with dignity. The court's view of Akbar also sent out a strong message to all men—no matter how powerful, wealthy and well-connected they may be, they were not above the law. The winds of change that Bhanwari Devi set in motion thirty years ago was turned into a storm by Ramani's victory. It is blowing through the nation as you read these words, and it is up to each of us, whatever gender we may be, to keep that mast of justice flying high.

THE RIGHT TO LOVE

Menaka Guruswamy

b. 1974

On the morning of 6 September 2018, millions of criminals in India were told by the Supreme Court that their punishment was over, that at last, after years of waiting, they were equal to any of their fellow citizens. Sounds fantastical, right? The Supreme Court, which is the highest court in the country, does have tremendous power, indeed, to pull off such magic. But actually, it needed years of efforts of brave and brilliant lawyers to persuade the judges of the court to do right by the people. Menaka Guruswamy, the hero of this chapter, is one among a team of such lawyers, who changed the lives of millions of Indians on that fateful day.

It was a moment of big hopes and big fears, but as five judges of the Supreme Court read out four verdicts on the cases Guruswamy and her colleagues were fighting, there was jubilation inside and outside the courtroom. People milled around the streets with rainbow flags, carried posters with victory slogans emblazoned on them. There was much singing and dancing, reciting of poetry and emotional speeches. People hugged one another, wept tears of joy and relief, they could dare to dream of a brighter future at long last.

There was good reason for making such a lot of fuss. India had finally got rid of a law that the British rulers had foisted on us more than 150 years ago as part of a penal code, which is a set of rules about the punishment to be given to anyone who commits a crime in this country. Lord Thomas Babington Macaulay, a British politician who, among other things, introduced the English language as a mode of communication in India, was one of the architects of this document.

Many of the laws he wrote down were influenced by the social and political climate of his time. Under the reign of Queen Victoria, when people followed strict rules of decorum in the way they conducted their lives, social and moral values were different from our time. The most obvious example is the treatment of women: not only were they considered inferior to men, but they had few rights, be it in exercising their right to vote or inheriting property.

One of the worst legacies of Lord Macaulay's penal code, however, was written into Section 377 of the document. The gist of this law, without going into the details of the jargon, stated that two people could not be allowed to be in love with each other, or in a romantic relationship, unless they were of different genders, that is one was a man and the other woman. Further, they should not behave in a way that was seen by society as 'unnatural'—even if they were doing so in the privacy of their homes. This law came into effect in 1860 and had its full run for 158 years, until it was struck down by the Supreme Court in 2018.

There are many people in this world who do not live by the usual norms set by society, when it comes to making personal choices. This is entirely fair since an individual's likes and dislikes cannot be dictated by the opinion of others. What is 'natural' to some, may seem completely 'unnatural' to others—and deciding right and wrong in such matters, we have little other than a set of arbitrary standards to go by. It would be as absurd as, say, putting a ban on vanilla ice cream just because majority of people in a country did not like the flavour!

By the same logic, while there are men and women all around us who fall in love, get married, have children and start a family, there are equally men who like to be with other men, and women who like women, and still others who are somewhere in between in their likes and preferences. People who do not obey the rules followed by the majority also want to be recognized by society, and to freely express their affection towards their partners. Then there are people who are born male or female but do not identify as one. Some change their names and gender from male to female, or female to male, as they grow older. The process involves painful and complex surgeries and procedures done to their bodies over months, to say nothing of the mental ups and downs they suffer in the process. There also are those who do not surgically alter their bodies but continue to behave and dress in a manner that expresses the way they feel about their gender identities.

Human beings are too diverse and wondrous to be slotted into the binary of male and female—just as a rainbow in the sky is made up of many colours, so are our

identities created out of many dreams and desires that
are fluid, and not always possible to categorize. If you do
not see such diversity of characters around you, or see
them rarely, it is only because society does not approve of
difference—you can even say society is *afraid* of difference
because it requires great courage to be able to live the
truth of who you are. It was on behalf of a handful of such
brave people, who fought for their individual rights and
on behalf of millions of others like them, that Guruswamy,
and a team of lawyers like Anand Grover, Arundhati
Katju and Saurabh Kirpal, appeared before India's highest
court in 2018.

Born in 1974, educated in India, Oxford and New York,
Guruswamy was already a well-known lawyer by this time.
Her practice, like that of many other lawyers, drew deeply
from the provisions already existing in the Constitution
of India. All citizens of India are promised equality and
liberty in the eyes of the law by this document, which
was drafted by Babasaheb Ambedkar, among others, soon
after the British left India. Born into a Dalit caste that has
suffered centuries of oppression (and still does), Ambedkar
was especially mindful that everyone in the country—
poor, illiterate, living on the margins or belonging to a
minority—was treated with the dignity and respect due
to every human being. And he ensured that this idea was
enshrined in the letter and spirit of the Constitution—that
is, not only was it recorded in the text of it, but the concept
of equality was also put in practice by India's courts.

Making a pledge on paper is easy, but turning it into
reality is a slow, uphill fight—one that requires years of
patience and persistence to change the mindset of a society

that is fixated on beliefs and value systems established through habit and tradition.

The LGBTQ+ community—the acronym is an umbrella term for Lesbian, Gay, Bisexual, Transgender, Queer and others who identify differently from society's idea of male and female—was (and continues to be) an easy target for people who like to boss over the private lives and choices of others. Although the Constitution is clear on protecting the rights of every citizen of India, the so-called 'moral guardians' of society like to think otherwise.

DID YOU KNOW?

The diversity and beauty of the LGBTQ+ community is represented by rainbow colours, as you may have seen in 'pride' marches, organized to celebrate the power of the community, with rainbow flags and banners carried by the participants. The term is an umbrella for lesbian (women who like women), gay (men who like men), bisexual (people who like both men and women), transgender (people who identify as a gender different from the one they were assigned at birth), queer (those who may identify as any one or more of the above, or have an identity that is fluid, not fixed for always). All the possible identities that we can imagine exist in a spectrum, like all the colours in the world are contained in the seven shades of a rainbow.

Once a person turns eighteen, they become an adult in the eyes of the law, and it is nobody's business then to interfere with who they love or want to spend their lives with—so long as the other person involved is also an adult, willing to be in the relationship and no harm is caused to anyone by either of them by exercising their respective choices. The idea may sound obvious, but the LGBTQ+ community has been suffering indignity and violence from society, especially from the police, for decades because of their desire to live life on their own terms.

The harassment and humiliation usually start early, at home or in schools, where a person is insulted for being too 'girly' or 'tomboyish'. (Think back for a moment if you have ever said such a word to another person, have been called it yourself or seen another person suffering at the hands of others?)

Such name-calling is partly the result of the assumption that there is a set of rules that regulate the way we ought to live out the gender assigned to us at birth. To a certain degree, it arises out of ignorance and fear of engaging with people who are different. Verbal abuse often turns into physical attack or, worse, small acts of daily aggression— such as sniggering behind the person's back, mimicking their body language, or excluding them from networks of family and friendship. It is like knowing all your classmates are having a party, but no one wants you around—just because you happen to like oranges when the rest of them like apples.

Before Guruswamy and her colleagues stepped into the courtroom to right these wrongs, thousands of others— activists, members of the LGBTQ+ community, friends and families who support them and ordinary citizens—have been fighting a pitched battle to get rid of Section 377. Initially, only a handful came out on the streets to claim their rights. India's first pride march was held in 1999, in Kolkata, with only fifteen participants. In the next ten years, the numbers began to swell, as other cities and towns began to host such gatherings. Then, a turning point came in 2009. In a landmark ruling that year, the Delhi High Court decided that the law, as it applied to LGBTQ+ people, violated the promise of equal treatment made to every Indian by the Constitution. Suddenly, the community saw a ray of hope, many found the courage to come of the 'closet', where they had locked up their deepest desires. But the triumph was brief.

Soon, an astrologer called Suresh Kumar Kaushal, backed by a group of religious leaders, appealed to the Supreme Court to reconsider the relevance of Section 377. In 2013, two judges of the court hearing the case decided that the law could stay. They argued that LGBTQ+ Indians were very few in number, and that their lives were barely affected by Section 377. If the law were to be removed, the judges added, it would have to be done by a vote by lawmakers in Parliament, not by the courts. It was an unrealistic hope because few members of Parliament were willing to put their necks out to fight for the rights of the LGBTQ+ community.

It was then that Guruswamy, her life partner and fellow lawyer Arundhati Katju, along with a few others, set out on their fight. They decided to file a petition with the Supreme Court, urging it to rethink its earlier ruling on Section 377, but went about it in a cleverly roundabout fashion. Instead of only sticking to the arguments they had in their legal arsenal, they decided to make an emotional appeal to the judges. To counter the belief stated by the earlier verdict—that LGBTQ+ people were only a small minority of the population and did not matter in the big picture— the lawyers got influential LGBTQ+ Indians from all walks of life to file appeals before the judges. From restaurant owner and chef Ritu Dalmia to hotelier Keshav Suri to dancer Navtej Singh Johar, a range of personalities came forward, with their stories of love and loss, suffering and joy. Guruswamy represented a group of petitioners from the Indian Institute of Technology-Delhi and argued their case passionately. The stakes were too high for all those involved, including for her and Katju, who were not only present in their professional capacity, but also as a couple, as proud members of the LGBTQ+ community.

The court's decision on that September morning in 2018 was a momentous one, not only for India but also for other countries that were once ruled by the British— Pakistan, Bangladesh, Myanmar, Malaysia, and so on— where laws like Section 377 still play havoc with the lives of LGBTQ+ people. Justice Indu Malhotra, one of the five judges who read out the verdict, went so far as to say that society owes the LGBTQ+ community an apology for mistreating them for decades. While the legal change in India has not yet led to similar developments in some of our neighbouring nations, the good fight waged by Guruswamy and her allies has strengthened the will of other lawyers to keep crusading for justice.

In India, too, the absence of Section 377 is only the first in a series of changes needed to give the LGBTQ+ community a life of dignity. As Guruswamy said in an interview, quoting the Nobel Prize-winning economist Amartya Sen, that it is all very well to ensure freedom for everyone, but people must also have the capability to exercise the freedom given to them. Our duty as a nation does not end with merely acknowledging that all citizens as equal in the eyes of law—rather, it begins there. The principle of equality should be applied to practical realities to have any meaning, especially for LGBTQ+ people.

Today, LGBTQ+ Indians are, by law, as equal as any citizen of the country. Yet, they do not have the right to marry the person of their choice or adopt a child. Those who identify as transgender have been legally clubbed as people of the 'third gender', though many of them do not want to identify as such. Rather, those who have transitioned from one gender to another want to be acknowledged as persons of their desired genders. Even though they now have the right to vote or contest polls, they do not have the right to marry and have a family. Society still refers to them as hijras and wrongly assumes that all transgender people dance and beg on the streets for a living—when, in real life, transgender people are all around us, working in offices, teaching in schools, driving buses, and so on.

In recent years, openly transgender people have begun to find work in government service and with multinational companies. Members of the LGBTQ+ community were always part of the workforce but were forced to hide their identities. With the changing times, some employers are making an effort to understand the needs of LGBTQ+ employees—they are accepting that it is not possible to leave a vital part of your identity at home and wear a mask when you are at work. Such a life would be as stressful as having to pretend that you like soccer when you actually like no sports at all!

DO YOU KNOW THESE PROMINENT TRANSGENDER INDIANS?

- Zainab Patel: A transgender woman, she has worked with the United Nations and currently holds a job in the corporate sector, working to get more people from the community into the workforce.

- Laxmi Narayan Tripathi: This Bharatnatyam dancer, actor and activist living in Mumbai has worked tirelessly with several NGOs, including her own called Astitva, for the rights of the transgender community.

- Aryan Pasha: A bodybuilder who has won prizes in several competitions, Aryan transitioned into a man at the age of nineteen. He adopted a new name and identity on paper and is now fighting to help others like him who do not identify with the gender they were given at birth come out and live a fulfilling life.

To be a good human being, we must own the truth of who we are—and lawyers like Guruswamy have made it a little easier for us to do so. This is but the beginning of a journey for LGBTQ+ Indians, and for India as a nation. In time, hopefully Guruswamy and her colleagues will be able to convince the government to allow LGBTQ+ Indians their right to marry people they want. Until that happens, and even after it does, all of us can play a role in making this country a better place for LGBTQ+ people to live in.

ABOLISHING THE DEATH PENALTY

Anup Surendranath

b. 1981

In stories of the past, be they from the pages of history textbooks or fictional tales, people who were seen as having done something grievously wrong are given exemplary punishment by just rulers—the most severe one being death. Over two thousand years ago, when Emperor Ashoka had his laws inscribed on massive stone pillars, included among them was the punishment of putting an offender to death—what we now call the death penalty—even though Ashoka is now remembered for his compassionate reign. Those who have read Lewis Carroll's nonsense fantasy, *Alice in Wonderland*, may remember the foul-tempered Queen of Hearts, whose reaction to anyone who annoys her is: 'Off with his (or her) head!'

Indeed, there was a time, not too long ago, when a supreme monarch could order anyone guilty of committing a crime to be executed by a variety of methods—from having their head cut off by the guillotine in France to injecting them with a lethal drug (in the US) to hanging them by the noose until they are dead (in many countries around the world, including India). But thankfully, most nations live by different rules in the twenty-first century.

Of the 195 countries in the world, 140 do not award the death penalty anymore, while most of the others use it sparingly. China, Saudi Arabia, Iran and Pakistan are still known to have a special fondness for this extreme form of punishment and usually lead the numbers. In India, for the last forty years, the death penalty has been given only in the 'rarest of rare cases' (see box). It is left to a judge, or a group of judges, to decide if a case qualifies as such. But even so, arriving at a decision can be tricky, given the number of conditions on which the verdict of a case hinges.

In independent India, before a person deemed guilty of a crime is punished, they must be given a fair trial in a court of law, including a chance to speak for themselves. They should have a lawyer to defend them before a judge. And, at the heart of all these processes, is the assumption that the police have conducted a thorough investigation and collected all the data and evidence required to establish the guilt of the person beyond a shadow of doubt. Too many boxes need to be checked, leaving no room for error, or else an innocent person may end up spending years in jail. At worst, they may lose their life.

The judicial process in India, as in any other country in the world, is far from flawless. The poor and the powerless live in mortal terror of the police. The media often reports of instances where the police pick up hapless innocents, take them to a lockup, torture them and force a confession out of them for crimes they have not committed—either to save the powerful or simply because they cannot be bothered to carry out a rigorous investigation. Such forced admissions of guilt is not considered valid in a court but, by the time these cases are heard—almost always in English, a language many people in India do not speak or even understand—it is usually too late for the victims to make an appeal for their innocence. So, often, they have no option but to accept the verdict delivered by the presiding judge or judges.

Sometimes, a person can become involved in a case by association. In 1984, after Prime Minister Indira Gandhi was assassinated by her Sikh bodyguards, one of the two culprits were shot dead on the scene, while the other was tried and hanged to death. Curiously, another person, called Kehar Singh, was also sent to the noose, for being a co-conspirator to the murder, though he did not play a direct role in it. This is not at all to say that real killers and other criminals are not apprehended by the police and correctly punished by the courts. But rather, these examples merely point out the slippery slope that judicial decisions often turn out be.

That India was aware of this danger since the early days of Independence is evident from the number of times it has revised its position on the death sentence. Until 1955, the courts were required to offer special reasons for giving the life sentence instead of the death penalty. Then, in 1973, they were asked to give special reasons for imposing the death sentence. And finally, in 1980, the Supreme Court decided that such a punishment can be imposed only in 'the rarest of rare cases'. In 2015, a report published by the Law Commission of India, headed by Justice A.P. Shah, recommended that the death penalty be abolished—except when it is awarded to persons involved in acts of terrorism or in crimes against the State.

Around ten years ago, lawyer Anup Surendranath was also struck by the possibility of such mistakes creeping into the judicial process, when he started thinking about the death penalty in present-day India. Born and schooled in Bangalore, he had attended law school in Hyderabad and Oxford, UK, where he got a doctorate degree. In 2012, he came back to India to start teaching at the National Law University in Delhi.

That year, the entire world was shaken by a horrendous attack on a young woman and her male friend in a bus by a group of men in Delhi. The victim, who was referred to as 'Nirbhaya' by the media, died of her injuries. Her tragic end inspired huge protests across the country and eventually led to major changes in the law. Of her six attackers, one died in jail while the case was being heard. Four others were sentenced to death and executed in 2020. The sixth, and last, one was a juvenile (below the age of eighteen) when he committed the crime and was released in 2015. Indian law prohibits juveniles from being given the death penalty.

The brutality of the Nirbhaya case, along with the spirited coverage it received in the media, led to a groundswell of support for death penalty for the offenders. Most people felt that a strong message needed to be sent out to prevent future occurrences of such crimes—nothing short of death would do. Sadly, nearly a decade later and after the death of five of the six offenders in the Nirbhaya case, girls and women in India are not any safer. In 2018, the country was rattled, once again, by gruesome attacks on two young women in Unnao and Kathua respectively. Stronger laws, to say nothing of the death penalty, have not been able to deter anyone from committing such crimes. Clearly, we need to go back to the origins of the problem rather than treat it with severity once it assails us.

Surendranath's interest in the death penalty, though, was first stoked by another case. In 2013, a Kashmiri separatist leader called Mohammed Afzal Guru was executed by the Indian state for his role in the attack on the national Parliament in 2001. After Pranab Mukherjee, who was then the President of India, rejected a plea to pardon his life, Guru was quickly executed within a week. His family was informed two days after his death of the execution.

At that time, Surendranath had started working on a project that would become the *India Death Penalty Report*, which was published in 2016, also known as Project 39A. 'We knew so little about prisoners who are on the death row—and we still continue to know so little,' he recently told me. 'Even gathering the information about prisoners on the death penalty and their families proved to be a huge challenge.'

Project 39A, led by Surendranath, is the result of work put in by many student volunteers, whose job was to go to jails all over the country and record the testimony of people living under the death row. Apart from recording the details of the crimes they are accused of having committed, each profile is meant to capture the state of mind of the person waiting to be either pardoned or finally sent to the gallows. The idea is not to argue for the guilt or innocence of the person, but rather to bring out the sheer barbarity involved in awarding a punishment like the death penalty. 'I felt that if common people had a chance to "see" and "hear" the realities of those on the death row, irrespective of if they actually committed the crime or not, it would move them on a different level,' he says. 'What does it mean to live with your life in someone else's hand—when you don't know if you are going to live to see another day?'

The most compelling case against the death penalty is that revenge does not serve any purpose. 'An eye for an eye will leave the whole world blind,' Mahatma Gandhi famously said. By killing a person who is convicted of committing a murder, the State commits another murder. You may argue that the purpose behind the two killings is different, but you have to agree that the result is the same in both cases: death. The faint silver lining is that the death penalty is not an absolute judgement—it can be changed to a lifelong sentence through appeals.

India has several kinds of court, arranged according to rank, with the Supreme Court at the top. If a lower court sentences a person to death, the ruling can be contested in the higher courts, right up to the Supreme Court. Unfortunately, the poor and powerless do not have the resources to fight their cases for years, even decades. In India, appeal processes are not only complicated but also require a good lawyer, who usually charges a high fee. Given the large backlog of cases, the courts take a long time to dispense justice. Often, a person waiting on death row dies waiting for their case to be resolved. Indian prisons are not the most hygienic or safe places in the world either. Apart from being infected with diseases, there is a danger of being attacked under custody, either by fellow inmates who have a history of violence or by the police themselves. Ram Singh, one of the accused in the Nirbhaya case, is believed to have died of suicide while he was held in custody in 2013.

Even if the Supreme Court upholds a death penalty, there is still a provision in the law to send the verdict for a presidential review. It is called a mercy petition, where the person who is sentenced requests the President to pardon them, citing specific reasons to do so. Although the President has the final say on the fate of the individual, he is not allowed to take a decision without consulting the government of the day. And since a government is run by political parties elected by the people, it tends to follow the public's mood. In the Nirbhaya judgement, for instance, most Indians were already enraged by the culprits and offered widespread support for the death penalty. It was highly unlikely that either the government or the President would have taken a different view in the matter.

Not all mercy petitions are dispensed swiftly, though. As Surendranath and his team found out, many prisoners of death row wait for years for closure on their cases. These are men and women who were the primary breadwinners of their families. Their indefinite imprisonment has left their loved ones struggling for food and sustenance, to say nothing of the stigma they face from society for being related to a convicted murderer. Apart from the sheer inhumanity of the eye-for-an-eye mentality, Surendranath believes that the death penalty fails to address the deeper ills of society. The death penalty is a cop out, giving the judicial system, along with the rest of us, the chance to wash our hands of uncomfortable truths that may explain (though do not justify) the causes behind a crime.

'None of us is born evil,' Surendranath said. 'Who we become is a product of our upbringing and the circumstances in which we live.' There was a time, not too far back in the past, when most schools in India thought it was acceptable to use corporal punishment—hitting students, imposing physical torture on them, publicly humiliating them. To this day, some schools follow these methods to discipline a so-called 'problem child'. But the root of problematic behaviour lies deeper, be it in a child or an adult, going back to the family environment they grow up in, experiences of trauma that stay with them and much more.

If a child has difficulties in learning, it is up to their teacher to either review their teaching methods or probe deeper into the causes behind the child's inability to pay attention to and pick up lessons. Just as a sound thrashing cannot make a maths genius out of a helpless child, the death penalty will not be able to remove evil from society. If it were so simple to erase crime, places like Saudi Arabia, where people are publicly beheaded or shot to death, would have become completely crime free.

The decision to impose the death penalty is the ultimate test of dignity—the State, the legal system, the victims' families and society at large are all made to confront the value they assign to human life. While the desire to punish a heinous criminal is understandable, the impulse to not pay them in their own coin is what keeps the rest of us human.

In 1991, then Prime Minister Rajiv Gandhi was assassinated in an explosion carried out by members of Liberation Tigers of Tamil Eelam (LTTE), a Sri Lankan terrorist outfit, in Chennai. Following the tragedy, twenty-six LTTE members, including a woman called Nalini Sriharan, the only surviving member of the five-people team who killed Rajiv Gandhi, were arrested, tried in a special court and sentenced to death. In 1999, the court confirmed the death sentences but Sonia Gandhi, Rajiv Gandhi's widow, made an appeal in 2000, asking for

Sriharan's life to be spared on humanitarian grounds because she had given birth to a daughter in prison. In 2008, Priyanka Gandhi Vadra, Rajiv Gandhi's daughter, met Sriharan in jail, where she continues to serve a life sentence.

Surendranath believes that India will eventually do away with the death penalty and the courts will have a big role in bringing about this change. It is impossible to predict how long it may take for it come through, but in the meantime, we can all do our bit to increase awareness about the need to remove it from a great civilization such as ours.

THE VICTIMS OF THE BHOPAL GAS TRAGEDY

Satinath Sarangi

b. 1954

Shortly after midnight on 3 December 1984, thousands of people in Bhopal, the capital of Madhya Pradesh, woke up feeling horribly unwell. Their eyes watering, unable to breathe, nauseous and dizzy, men, women and children began to spill out of their homes in panic. There was poison in the air, but no one, including the doctors at the local hospitals, seemed to know what it was, or a way to escape its deadly clutches. Minutes of senseless terror turned into hours of agony, before it became clear that there was a leak at the local pesticide factory, owned by a US company called Union Carbide Corporation (UCC). A faulty system had caused a toxic gas called methyl isocyanate, or MIC, to be released into the air, which was the source of all this distress.

Two days after this event, when thousands of people were still struggling to make sense of the calamity that had visited them, a young man called Satinath Sarangi, called Sathyu by friends and colleagues, landed up in the city. Thirty years old at the time, Sathyu was a mechanical engineer, working on a PhD degree. When the gas leak took place, he happened to be nearby, volunteering with an NGO, helping farmers and tribal communities fight for their rights. Shocked by the reports coming out of Bhopal, he decided to make a brief visit to see if he could do anything for the victims. When he stepped outside the railway station, Sathyu was shaken by the scenes he saw around him. People wept and mourned, still in the grip of fear, struck as much by grief as by a sense of helplessness. Children and adults of shorter height were the worst affected, since MIC, which is heavier than air, tends to linger close to the ground level. Those who had cars or other means of transport fled to higher ground and were relatively safer. The survivors showed signs of lung damage, loss of eyesight and organ failure, for which there seemed to be no proper treatment. Piles of dead bodies were cremated together, even as the volunteers tried their best to comfort and console the ones who were alive and suffering.

A few days later, most of the volunteers left, as did thousands of local residents, fearing for their lives. But Sathyu, who had gone to Bhopal thinking he would spend a week or so helping with relief work, ended up staying for good, bidding goodbye to his doctoral research and the career that would have followed it. Instead, he decided to devote all his energies to helping the victims and survivors of the gas tragedy.

Sathyu filed compensation claims on their behalf, from UCC as well as the governments of Madhya Pradesh and India. He steered the poor and unlettered through the complex legal system in the hope that one day it may bring them a sense of justice and some closure. Yet, almost forty years later, the people of Bhopal, whose lives were destroyed in the gas leak, still bear the additional indignity of being victims of neglect by the Indian state and big corporations.

Although the government charged Warren Anderson, the chief of UCC in 1984, and put him in custody soon after the tragedy, he was allowed to return home to the US a few hours later. In 1992, after repeatedly failing to get him back to India, the courts declared him 'a fugitive from justice', that is, a person fleeing from the law. By the time Anderson died in 2014, at the ripe old age of ninety-two, the law was nowhere closer to getting hold of him. Although UCC paid compensation to the victims, the company insisted that the 1984 accident was due to the fault of its Indian employees. Later, after Dow, a chemical company that makes Eveready battery among other things, took over UCC, it refused to take any responsibility for the gas leak. The big multinational corporations may have washed their hands off the tragedy, but Sathyu's fight never lost its bite—he continues to work tirelessly for the victims and survivors to this day.

Although it might seem as though the disaster barely took a few hours to unfold, the Bhopal gas tragedy was a long time in the making. In the late 1960s, when UCC opened its pesticide factory in Bhopal, there was hope among the locals of more jobs coming up. In the initial years after setting up its operations, UCC circulated safety pamphlets among employees and the neighbouring hospitals, advising them on the steps to follow in case of a gas leak. But these manuals were written in English, a language which many people did not read or know well. Soon, as business started to falter, UCC's attention to processes also took a dive. The company felt cutting back on its losses was more important than improving its security standards. The result of this neglect began to show soon.

In 1976, a worker was accidentally exposed to phosgene, another toxic gas. Not knowing what to do, he panicked and took off his gas mask. Within three days, he was dead. Another incident, in 1982, saw twenty-four workers coming in contact with hazardous materials on the site. None of them were wearing the recommended protective equipment.

In the lead up to the 1984 gas leak, the refrigeration system needed to cool the gas tanks in case of overheating was believed to have been switched off to save power. Worse, some believed the leak was a deliberate act of sabotage by a worker who was unhappy with the management. The logbook showed the machines had remained unattended for some time that night between a change in the duty shift. So, it was possible for someone to tamper with the systems in secret. An employee of UCC also told the police that he had informed his managers about the leak as soon as he spotted it. But his seniors did not pay any heed and decided to attend to the situation half an hour later, after they were done with their tea break. By then, it was too late—MIC had poisoned the air and was burning through people's eyes and lungs all around.

Since decades have passed and many books, reports and surveys have appeared on the tragedy, it is not possible to summarize all its twists and turns the investigations have taken in one short chapter. But the human suffering is there for us to see—in the unforgettable photographs taken by Pablo Bartholomew and Raghu Rai, both of whom went on to win major awards for their work in Bhopal, and the lingering health problems that still afflict the people who continue to live in the area. Most of all, Sathyu's spirited activism on behalf of the victims and the survivors has not allowed their tragedy to be wiped off the public's memory. From time to time, he has organized non-violent protest marches, one involving walking even as far as Delhi. In 2011, a rail roko andolan—to halt the running of trains—to protest against the injustice done to the victims of the gas tragedy saw women and men being badly beaten up by the police. This, even after Sathyu and his comrades had informed the public of their plan days in advance so as not to cause them any inconvenience. Governments have come and gone, memorials for the victims of the gas tragedy have received more attention than compensating them for their losses, and the fight to give them a life of dignity is on till this day.

The Bhopal gas tragedy is a continuing saga because the effects of the leak did not only affect people back then, but also the generations that came after them. If MIC crosses the lung barrier and enters the bloodstream, it can play havoc with cells and chromosomes, the building blocks of life. As a result, children have been born with the scars of their parents' ordeals, many of them suffering from chronic headaches. Babies have died within years due to brain damage; some have not spoken a word for the first several years of their lives. The elderly have got cancer and lung disease; adults have become physically impaired. This cycle of trauma goes on because the area around the abandoned factory is still a dump of hazardous toxic material. The waterbodies and soil around the place are so badly laced with poisonous chemicals that humans and animals who have come in contact with them have developed chronic health problems. Fish have died and cattle become ill after drinking from nearby water systems.

A journalist from a US magazine visited the site in 2018 and found shining drops of mercury, which is extremely poisonous to humans and animals above a certain level, on the ground. She saw boys playing cricket on the site, some hanging out casually in the adjoining areas. In spite of it being a dangerous dumpyard full of lethal chemicals, people continue to live around the area, and keep getting ill with diseases like cancer—not by choice, of course, but because they have no means of moving to a safer neighbourhood.

Over the years, along with Sathyu, local residents and activists like Rasheeda Bi, Champa Devi Shukla, Abdul Jabbar and Rachna Dhingra have fought for justice for those affected by the gas leak. Apart from moving court and taking their demands to politicians, these enterprising individuals have also undertaken much-needed practical initiatives to help people on the ground. For instance, in 1996, Sathyu and his friends opened Sambhavna Trust Clinic, also known as Bhopal People's Health Documentation Clinic. It is an independent and community-based organization, run by social workers and doctors with the help of funds from individual donors, outside the interference of the government.

The Hindi word sambhavna is a made of two parts, sama (equal) and bhavna (feelings); together, it means 'to feel equally with others'. The aim of the project is to extend a helping hand to the residents around the UCC factory and figure out a long-term welfare plan that will help them live with dignity and improve their health. To this end, Sambhavna Trust, which has a garden rich with herbal plants and shrubs on its premises, uses a combination of traditional and modern medicinal treatments. From ayurveda to unani, it uses a variety of homegrown methods to treat patients, as well as yoga to heal the scars left on the minds of the survivors. Since respiratory

illnesses are common, yoga also helps improve breathing
and lung health. Such alternative healthcare is also a way
of countering the treatment available at local hospitals.
Since most of the doctors are unaware of the best way to
deal with MIC poisoning, the medicines they give tend
to be symptomatic—that is only meant to cure or control
a few symptoms instead of removing the root of the
problem. And so, pharmaceutical companies, sensing an
opportunity to make big money, have hiked up the prices
of allopathic drugs used to treat survivors. By providing
free treatment to those registered as gas-affected people
until 1986, the Sambhavna Trust tries to break this chain
of exploitation by big companies.

Putting a number to the victims of the Bhopal gas leak
is tricky and fraught with moral dilemmas. At what point
is it all right to stop counting the affected, since the Bhopal
gas tragedy is a continuing disaster, with defects and
ailments passed down from one generation to the next?
Is there ever going to be an end to this saga of suffering?
Various government bodies have put the number of
victims to around 5000, but the number is disputed by
NGOs who have worked on the ground. Some estimate as
many as 25,000 people were affected by the gas leak.

Then there is the bigger question of money. How
much of it can compensate for the loss of loved ones,
the disabilities of those left alive and the destruction
of the health and happiness of families? What kind of
inheritance are the victims and survivors leaving behind
for their children, who are born into a tragedy with no
end in sight? Even as we struggle to wrap our heads
around these questions and brave people like Sathyu wage
wars against big corporations and corrupt governments,

events like Bhopal gas tragedy continue to take place all over the world.

DID YOU KNOW?

- In 1986, a nuclear reactor accident in Chernobyl, Ukraine, left thousands dead or with life threatening diseases. The region saw a spike in children getting cancer, while deadly radioactive rays left a toxic footprint far into Europe.

- In 2011, the world was rocked by another nuclear tragedy, this time in Fukushima in Japan, where a nuclear power plant exploded after a major earthquake and tsunami.

- More recently, in May 2020, a dozen people died and about one thousand fell sick after a gas leak from LG Polymers chemical plant in the southern city of Visakhapatnam in India. This time, the gas released was styrene, which also causes damage to the respiratory system and can lead to lifelong disabilities.

Thirty-six years have passed since the Bhopal gas tragedy—yet its trail of suffering has far from ended. Since its founding in 1996, the Sambhavna Trust Clinic has treated more than 25,000 people. A majority of them show signs of damage to vital organs, including widespread disorder of the thyroid gland and chronic obesity. Being overweight puts people more at risk of diabetes, heart disease, different types of cancer, high blood pressure and other diseases. For instance, when the Covid-19 pandemic struck, Sambhavna Trust noted that the coronavirus killed victims of the gas tragedy in greater numbers than the rest of the population around Bhopal. It led to a fresh demand for compensation to be given to these people, including candle marches, but without much effect.

Until the state stops looking at victims of large-scale industrial disasters as just numbers and big corporations learn to control their greed, such incidents are going to happen in different parts of the world. But the silver lining will always be the presence of bravehearts like Sathyu—and the hope that their work will continue to inspire others to come forward to fight for a safer world.

BELIEF IN ABILITY

Mahantesh GK
b. 1970

It is the early 1970s, and the scene is Sisiri, a farming
village in Belgaum district of Karnataka in the south
of India. A small boy is sitting on the last bench of a
classroom in the village school, listening carefully to
everything that is being taught through the day. Even
though the teachers have not admitted him to the school,
merely allowed him to sit in on the lessons, the boy is
remarkably bright. Like a sponge, he absorbs everything
he hears. Soon, he is able to work out maths problems
orally. By the age of six, he is reciting tables up to 250.
But it won't be until the age of ten that he would get to
attend a school formally. For that to happen, he would
have to travel a long distance, to the big city of Bengaluru,
the capital of his state, with his parents, who will find a
special school for him to fit into. Meet Mahantesh GK,
who was once this little boy and is now a pioneer among
changemakers in India.

Mahantesh was the much-adored first child of a joint
family of thirty people. In the months leading up to his
birth in 1970, the ancestral home in the village was given a
grand makeover, decorated all over to welcome the arrival

of the baby. But along with boundless happiness, the boy also brought great sorrow. When he was six months old, Mahantesh caught typhoid, a terrible disease that took away his eyesight.

In India, millions of children are born with disabilities or become disabled during the course of their lives. These could be blindness, loss of speech and hearing, or any other physical deformity. In 2011, when the government ran a census in which they counted the population of the country, the number of Indians living with disabilities was found to be around twenty-one million—though activists and social workers believe the actual figure to be as high as sixty to seventy million. Most of these people belong to the poorer sections of society or, even if they don't, they mostly do not get the kind of support and opportunities they need to enjoy a full life.

Luckily for Mahantesh, his family loved and cared for him dearly. They never doubted for a moment that he deserved the best chances, like any child, to make a mark for himself. So his parents sent Mahantesh to a school for children with special needs in Bengaluru, where he performed well, and especially shone as a cricketer.

Cricket was an early love for the young boy, since the time he lived in the village. In those days, television was yet to arrive in India, but people loyally listened to the radio. Little Mahantesh was inseparable from the transistor, which became his best buddy, especially when a cricket match was on. He would listen to the commentary with rapt attention and even picked up a working knowledge of English from it. At his school in Bengaluru, he pursued his love for the game by playing it himself. Eventually, his sporting talent would take him to England on a tour with the blind cricket team in 1998. None of this would have been possible without the excellent support system of Mahantesh's family and, later on, his teachers, who never made him feel limited by his blindness.

It is no surprise that as Mahantesh grew older he wanted to extend the opportunities he was fortunate enough to get himself to millions of others like him—not only to people who were visually challenged but also to others with different disabilities. So, along with his close friend L Nagesh, Mahantesh started an association of blind cricketers. They formulated special rules and created customized equipment for this version of the game. In 2011, the Indian blind men's national cricket team was formed by the Cricket Association for the Blind in India (CABI), which is affiliated to the World Blind Cricket Council (WBCC). Mahantesh would head both CABI and WBCC.

MEET THE GAMECHANGERS!

- The national blind cricket teams, for men and women, is run by CABI. Both teams play One Day Internationals (ODI) and T20 matches. The men's team won the T20 World Cup in 2012 by defeating Pakistan. In 2014, they won the ODI World Cup against the two-time world champions Pakistan.

- The men's team also defeated Pakistan in the 2018 World Cup finals in Sharjah and the T20 World Cup final in Bengaluru in 2017. Both times, the team was led by Ajay Kumar Reddy, the young and charismatic skipper, who is a right-arm fast bowler.

- While blind women's cricket teams have existed alongside male teams in some parts, the Karnataka blind women's cricket team was founded as recently as 2019. The girls, selected and trained in a few short weeks from different parts of the state, quickly picked up the game, which was completely new to some of them, and emerged as runners-up in the national championship in New Delhi later that year.

You might wonder why Mahantesh focused on cricket, when there are so many other ways in which blind people can be helped. But the question to ask is, why not cricket? Why should physical disability come in the way of a person's right to do what they love and is good at? As Mahantesh has repeatedly said over the years, we must believe in a person's ability, instead of judging them only in terms of their disability. 'It is our inability that doesn't identify talent in disabled people,' as he put it. The right to play a sport should be part of a disabled person's life opportunities as anyone else's.

Through his personal experience of growing up as a person with disability (also sometimes referred to in short as PwD), Mahantesh was keenly aware of the problems that ran through Indian society. The biggest hurdle was an attitude of easy negativity that no one seemed to be bothered by too much. Even if parents wanted to admit their child with a disability to a regular school, the standard response from the school authorities was a loud no. Why? Because their school did not have the right set-up for children with special needs. The same logic was repeated by companies and workplaces—their offices did not have the facilities to fit in disabled workers. The obvious response would be: If you do not have the facilities, such as toilets, that a disabled person can use, you should build them! The same goes for desks, chairs and other disabled-friendly furniture. If your building does not have a ramp to enable access to people in wheelchairs, it's time to change the design. And last, but not least, if an activity requires speech, sight or hearing, faculties that a disabled person may lack, invest in and build new technologies to solve the problem! After all, technology, as Mahantesh said in a TEDx talk, does not discriminate among people; it is only human beings who do so.

Simple as these solutions may sound, they are far from easy to implement, because to do so would involve changing the mindset of the majority of society, and that, as we know from the other chapters in this book, requires years of devoted activism. So, in 1997, Mahantesh established Samarthanam Trust, an organization that would work with PwDs to nurture and nourish their dreams and desires. Samarthanam is especially alert that the problem almost always starts with low self-esteem felt by a PwD, who has perhaps not been loved enough or treated with the dignity and compassion they deserve by their families and society. Samarthanam aims to nurture and nourish the talents that PwDs may have kept to themselves, out of fear or diffidence, and identify the spark that makes each of them gifted in one thing or the other. The Trust is particularly attentive to the needs of young women with disabilities, who tend to be neglected and seen as a burden on their family's resources.

Samarthanam's vision for change goes far beyond making sports accessible. It has invested in creating a computer laboratory equipped with technology that converts text to speech to help train the sightless. Other vocational projects like Kirana, a rural call centre to help businesses, have helped generate job opportunities for at least a hundred rural blind and disabled youth. Thanks to the persistence of the Trust, blind students have gone on to join MBA courses all around the country and qualified as chartered accountants. Through a combination of sports and training people for suitable jobs, Samarthanam has created potential tax-paying citizens out of PwDs, instead of leaving them dependent on the charity of society. This was Mahantesh's long-cherished dream—with each passing year it is growing bigger.

But not all is well for PwDs in India, of course. Ask yourself, how many friends with a disability do you have? Have you ever had such a student in your class? Do you see many PwDs working in banks, hotels, supermarkets and other businesses around you? If there are some seventy million PwDs living in India today (the number is likely to be more rather than less as ten years have passed since the last census), why do we see so few of them working in regular jobs? Their relative absence is especially striking considering that the law allows for a quota of jobs to be reserved for PwDs.

A big reason for such invisibility is our country's mindset, which is far from reformed as far as PwDs are concerned. This, in spite of a strong legal framework that supports their rights to equal opportunities and guarantees them protection from abuse and discrimination. In real life, it often doesn't have the desired effect. Some years ago, a young disability activist called Virali Modi, who was a runner-up at the Miss Wheelchair contest (a beauty contest for women with disabilities), started an online campaign to urge prime minister Narendra Modi to make the Indian Railways user-friendly for PwDs. Harassed by the porters who had to carry her around during one journey, Virali Modi realized that starting with the height of the carriage (with no wheelchair ramp attached to it) to the design of the toilets inside trains that most PwDs won't be able to use, the entire experience was a nightmare for a person like her, who has to use a wheelchair. Add to it, the hostility and indifferent stares of fellow passengers, and the ordeal feels even worse.

Before Virali Modi's campaign made news, a para-athlete (an athlete with disabilities) was forced to sleep on the floor of a compartment of a train because she was allotted an upper berth, against the law, which she couldn't climb up. In yet another incident, disability activist Kuhu Das, who wears metal clippers because of her polio since a young age, was asked to take off these braces at security check-in at Kolkata airport. The police officer in charge remained fixated on her demand even after being told that complying with such a request would involve Das taking off her trousers in public! Das's fellow traveller, Jeeja Ghosh, another disability activist who has travelled all over the world for her work in spite of being afflicted with cerebral palsy, was told that she would not be able to fly unless she was accompanied by an able-bodied attendant. Not only were these experiences enraging and humiliating for Das and Ghosh, but also blatantly against the law, which protects PwDs from such insensitive behaviour.

In the twenty-first century, India's attitude to PwDs leaves much to be desired, especially as we like to fancy ourselves as a regional superpower. What good is a country that does not treat a sizable section of its population with dignity and respect?

Seventeen years after Mahantesh's birth, a baby was born to parents in New Delhi in 1987, looking blue, bleeding and with his arms and legs fractured. The worried parents took him from doctor to doctor, who could not diagnose what was wrong with the boy. One even described him as a 'wooden doll'. Eventually, they figured out that their son, who they named Nipun Malhotra, was born with a rare defect that does not allow the muscles in his arms and legs to develop, leaving him disabled for life and dependent on a wheelchair.

Nipun's parents refused to resign themselves to fate and decided to send their son to a regular school. Even though he did not make a single friend during his school years and his mother would sit next to him in class, taking notes on his behalf and protecting him from bullies, Nipun went on to perform brilliantly in his school-leaving examinations. On his wheelchair, he travelled everywhere, attended St Stephen's College in Delhi, followed by the Delhi School of Economics and Indian School of Business. But even after such enviable achievements, Nipun found himself without a job. His CV would be praised and shortlisted for interviews, but the moment he entered the room, everyone's face would fall. The interviewers would be busy coming up with excuses for not offering him the job he badly wanted. As the situation did not seem to improve, Nipun slid into depression, which was when his family took matters in their hand and decided to help him start his own venture.

Today the boy who was once called a 'wooden doll' heads an enterprise called the Nipman Foundation and runs a project called Wheels for Life, a platform where donations are raised from people to help buy wheelchairs for those who need but cannot afford them. Nipun is also a writer, speaker and advocate for disability rights, who travels all over the world speaking about his journey. The Nipman Foundation, according to Nipun, tries to create conditions that would allow PwDs to lead productive and happy lives. For a recent project, he worked with Zomato, the food delivery and hospitality company, to make wheelchair access a part of their restaurant listing on the app. Why should PwDs not enjoy eating out like everyone else?

'A person's disability exists in terms of the barriers in society,' Nipun said in a 2017 interview. The same sentiment lies at the core of Mahantesh's work, too, who helped modify the standard cricket ball to make it sound like a rattle that would enable blind players to take part in the sport. To remove barriers not only do we need people like Malhotra and Mahantesh, but also others, who are not disabled but just as invested in creating an inclusive world, where everyone, irrespective of their ability, is treated with dignity and compassion—and given every opportunity to realize their dreams.

Before You Go ...

Thank you for reading this book till the end!

If you want to know more about these heroes, here are some resources for you.

Irom Sharmila

- There are many books on Irom Sharmila in various Indian languages, but one of the best-known ones is *Burning Bright: Irom Sharmila and the Struggle for Peace in Manipur* (Penguin India, 2009) by Deepti Priya Mehrotra.
- Some of Irom Sharmila's poems written in Meiteilon, her mother tongue, have been translated and collected in *Fragrance of Peace* (Zubaan, 2010).

Aruna Roy

- The best account of the right to information movement is in *The RTI Story: Power to the People* (Roli Books, 2018), written by Aruna Roy with the MKSS collective.
- If you wish to get a quick snapshot of the movement, you can listen to Aruna Roy and Nikhil Dey speak about it at an event titled, 'The Anatomy of a People's Movement', organized by Skoll Foundation in 2010, which is available to stream on YouTube: https://www.youtube.com/watch?v=TXP_eO5Th50

Bezwada Wilson

- Although there aren't books written about Bezwada Wilson yet, you can find some of his talks online. I especially recommend one called 'The Right to Human Dignity', a TEDx event you can stream on YouTube: https://www.youtube.com/watch?v=SJ30BrF3EBc
- One of the most moving accounts of B.R. Ambedkar's life and work can be found in *Bhimayana: Experiences of Untouchability* (Navayana, 2011), which has artwork and texts by Durgabai Vyam, Srividya Natrajan, Subhash Vyam and S. Anand.

Medha Patkar

- One of the early chronicles of the Narmada Bachao Andolan is in *A Narmada Diary*, a documentary movie made by Simantini Dhuru and Anand Patwardhan in 1995.
- Subhadra Sen Gupta's book, *Caring for Nature: The River of Life* (TERI Press, 2016), tells the story of the Narmada Bachao Andolan for young readers.

Dr Devi Shetty

- The most comprehensive overview of Dr Shetty's life and career that I have drawn from is in the episode on him in the documentary mini-series, *The Surgeon's Cut*, which you can watch on Netflix.

Bhanwari Devi

- Bhanwari Devi's life inspired the movie, *Bawandar* (2000), directed by Jag Mundhra, with Nandita Das playing Saanvri, the character based on her.
- Aparna Jain writes about Bhanwari Devi's courage in her illustrated book, *Like A Girl: Real Stories for Tough Kids* (Westland, 2018).

Menaka Guruswamy

- There are many movies in different Indian languages that revolve around the lives of the LGBTQ+ community. A recent example, one that has a happy ending, is *Shubh Mangal Zyada Saavdhan*, starring Ayushmann Khurrana and Jitendra Kumar.
- Many books for young readers increasingly feature LGBTQ+ characters. One of my favourites is the picture book, *Guthli Has Wings* (Tulika, 2019), by author and illustrator Kanak Shashi.

Anup Surendranath

- *Abolishing the Death Penalty: Why India Should Say No to Capital Punishment* by Gopal Krishna Gandhi (Aleph Book Company) is a useful introduction to the subject.
- *The Punished: Stories of Death-Row Prisoners* by Jahnavi Misra, co-written with Project 39A (HarperCollins India), retells the stories of some of India's death-row prisoners as they await the end of their roads.

Satinath Sarangi

- *Bhopal Gas Tragedy* (Tulika, 2005) by Suroopa Mukherjee gives an overview of the crisis and the years of activism carried out by Sathyu and his comrades.
- In a TEDx talk given at IIM Kozhikode, Sathyu recounts four key stories from Bhopal that throw light on the gas disaster and its aftermath. You can find the video recording of it on YouTube: https://www.youtube.com/watch?v=wmWcEYufQsc

Mahantesh GK

- You can hear Mahantesh's life story in his own words in the many talks he has given. I would particularly recommend this TEDx Talk, which is available on YouTube: https://www.youtube.com/watch?v=8-Z86aVooCc
- There are many books on disability in India. A recent one is *Grit: The Major Story* (Hachette India, 2019) by Major Devender Pal Singh, who is a war veteran, India's first blade runner and a motivational speaker.
- Nipun Malhotra has a section on his website (https://www.nipunmalhotra.com/videos), where he shares various video appearances, whether they are talks, interviews or even comic skits. You will learn a lot from watching them—and have a lot of fun too!

Somak Ghoshal grew up in Kolkata, went to college in Oxford, then worked in Delhi. Currently, he lives in Bengaluru with his teddy bear, who has been his best friend for thirty-five years and writes about books, art and people who are fighting to right wrongs. He is a cat person, who also loves dogs and ice cream. His picture book *Piku's Little World*, illustrated by Proiti Roy, was published by Pratham Books in 2019.